"I'm sorry we won't be working together any longer, Jaya."

"Thank you." She swallowed and wondered if she would turn into a complete fool and start to cry. Standing, she put her hand in his and tried for one firm shake.

Theo kept her hand. His thumb grazed over the backs of her knuckles.

Her skin tingled and her stomach took a rollercoaster dip and swoop.

She looked at his eyes, but he was looking at their hands. Her fingers quivered in his grip as he turned her palm up. She almost thought he was going to raise it to his lips.

It was Theo's eyes, Theo's expression that was always so aloof, but now it glowed with something that was aggressive and hungry.

He was going to kiss her!

She stiffened with apprehension and he straightened. Her hand wound up hanging in the air ungrasped as he pulled in a strained breath.

"This is not appropriate. I apologize."

"No, I—" *Please* let her dark skin disguise some of these fervent blushes. "You surprised me. I came in here reminding myself not to call you Theo. I didn't think you thought about me like that. I would—"

Was she really going to risk this? She had to. She'd never get another chance.

"I'd like it if you kissed me."

Dani Collins discovered romance novels in high school and immediately wondered how a person trained and qualified for *that* amazing job. She married her high school sweetheart, which was a start, then spent two decades trying to find her fit in the wide world of romance writing—always coming back to Harlequin Mills & Boon® Modern™ Romance.

Two children later, and with the first entering high school, she placed in Harlequin's *Instant Seduction* contest. It was the beginning of a fabulous journey towards finally getting that dream job.

When she's not in her Fortress of Literature, as her family calls her writing office, she works, chauffeurs children to extra-curricular activities, and gardens with more optimism than skill.

Dani can be reached through her website at www.danicollins.com

Recent titles by the same author:

A DEBT PAID IN PASSION
MORE THAN A CONVENIENT MARRIAGE
PROOF OF THEIR SIN
NO LONGER FORBIDDEN?

Did you know these are also available as eBooks?
Visit www.millsandboon.co.uk

AN HEIR
TO BIND THEM

BY
DANI COLLINS

Published in Great Britain 2014
by Mills & Boon, an imprint of Harlequin (UK) Limited,
Eton House, 18-24 Paradise Road, Richmond, Surrey, TW9 1SR

ISBN: 978 0 263 24238 6

Harlequin (UK) Limited's policy is to use papers that are natural,
renewable and recyclable products and made from wood grown in
sustainable forests. The logging and manufacturing processes conform
to the legal environmental regulations of the country of origin.

Printed and bound in Spain
by CPI Antony Rowe, Chippenham, Wiltshire

AN HEIR
TO BIND THEM

This one's for my kids,
who managed to turn out amazing despite having a
writer for a mom. Or should I say not having a mom?

I often joke that our daughter
has done a marvelous job raising our son.
For that, and all the times Delainey made lunch
for Sam (and me) so I could write, I am deeply grateful.

I also owe a very special thanks to Sam
for his suggestion when I had ten thousand words to go
on this manuscript and I was stuck. He said, "Dude..."
(Yes, he calls me Dude, but this dude looks like a lady.)
"Dude, have the brother tell her something she doesn't
know about the hero." Post-secondary tuition saved!

PROLOGUE

THEO MAKRICOSTA BLINKED sweat out of his eyes as he glanced between his helicopter's fuel gauge and the approaching shoreline. He was a numbers man so he didn't worry at times like this; he calculated. His habit was to carry twice the fuel needed for any flight. He'd barely touched down on the yacht before he'd been airborne for his return trip. A to B equaled B to A, so he should have enough.

Except in this case *B* stood for *boat,* which was a moving point.

And he'd made a split-second decision as he lifted off the *Makricosta Enchantment* to go to Marseille rather than back to Barcelona. It had been an instinct, the type of impulse that wasn't like him at all, but uncharacteristic panic had snared him in those first few seconds as he took flight. He had wheeled the bird toward what felt like salvation.

It had been a ludicrous urge, but he was committed now.

And soaked in perspiration.

Not that he was worried for his own life. He wouldn't be missed if he dropped out of the sky. But his cargo would. The pressure to safeguard his passengers had him so tense he was liable to snap his stick.

It didn't help that despite the thump of the rotors and his earmuffs plugged into the radio, he could hear both babies screaming their lungs out. He already sucked at being a brother. Now he might literally go down in flames as an uncle. Good thing he'd never tried fatherhood.

Swiping his wet palm on his thigh, he pulled his phone from his pocket. Texting and flying was about as smart as texting while driving, but if he managed to land safely, he would have a fresh host of problems to contend with. His instincts in heading north instead of west weren't *that* far off. The perfect person to help him was in Marseille.

If she'd help him.

He called up the message he should have deleted a long time ago.

This is my new number, in case that's the reason you never called me back. Jaya.

Ignoring the twist of shame the words still wrung out of his conscience, he silently hoped her heart was as soft as he remembered it.

CHAPTER ONE

Eighteen months ago...

JAYA POWERS HEARD the helicopter midmorning, but Theo Makricosta still hadn't called her by five, when she was technically off the clock. Off the payroll in fact, and leaving in twelve hours.

Ignoring the war between giddiness and heartache going on in her middle, she reminded herself that normal hours of work didn't confine Mr. Makricosta. He traveled so much that sometimes he couldn't sleep, so he worked instead. If he wanted files or records or reports, he called despite the time and politely asked her for them. Then he reminded her to put in for lieu or overtime and thanked her for her trouble. He was an exceptionally good man to work for and she was going to miss him way beyond what was appropriate.

Staring at herself in the mirror, packed bags organized behind her, she wondered why she was still dressed in her Makricosta Resort uniform. She gave herself a pitying headshake. Her hair was brushed and restored to its heavy bun, her makeup refreshed, her teeth clean. All in readiness for his call.

After everything that had sent her running from her home in India, she never would have seen herself turning into this: a girl with a monumental crush on her boss.

Did he know she was leaving and didn't care? He'd never

overstepped into personal, ever. If he had any awareness that she was a woman, she'd be shocked.

That thought prompted her to give a mild snort. If she hadn't seen him buy dinner for the occasional single, vacationing woman, always accompanying her back to her room then subsequently writing off her stay against his personal expense account, she'd have surmised he wasn't aware of women at all.

But he hooked up when it suited him and it made her feel…odd. Aware and dismayed and kind of jealous.

Which was odd because *she* didn't want to sleep with him. Did she?

A flutter of anxious tension crept from her middle toward her heart. It wasn't terror and nausea, though. It wasn't the way she typically felt when she thought of sex.

It wasn't fireworks and shooting stars, either, so why did she care that she might not have a chance to say goodbye?

Her entire being deflated. She had to say goodbye. It wasn't logical to feel so attached to someone who'd been nothing but professional and *de*tached, but she did. The promotions and career challenges alone had made him a huge part of her life, whether his encouragement had been personal or not. More importantly, the way he respected her as useful and competent had nurtured her back to feeling safe in her workplace again. He made her feel like maybe, just maybe, she could be a whole woman, rather than one who had severed herself from all but the most basic of her female attributes.

Did she want to tell him that? *No.* So forget it. She would leave for France without seeing him.

But rather than unknotting her red-and-white scarf, her hand scooped up her security card. She pivoted to the door. Stupid, she told herself as she walked to the elevator. What if he was with someone?

A few minutes later she swiped her damp palms on her

skirt before knocking on his door. Technically this for-
tieth floor villa belonged to the Makricosta family, but
the youngest brother, Demitri, wasn't as devoted to duty
as Theo, flitting through on a whim and only very sel-
dom. Their sister, Adara, the figurehead of the operation,
timed her visits to catch a break from New York winters,
not wasting better July weather elsewhere when it was its
coolest here in Bali.

Theo—Mr. Makricosta, she reminded herself, even
though she thought of him as Theo—was very methodi-
cal, inspecting the books of each hotel in the chain at least
once a quarter. He was reliable and predictable. She liked
that about him.

Licking her lips, she knocked briefly.

The murmur inside might have been "Come in." She
couldn't be sure and she had come this far, so she used
her card and—

"I said, *Not now*," he stated from a reclined position on
the sofa, shirt sleeves rolled up and one bare forearm over
his eyes. In the other hand he held a drink. His jaw was
stubbled, his clothes wrinkled. Papers and file folders were
strewn messily across the coffee table and fanned in a wide
scatter across the floor, as though he'd thrust them away in
an uncharacteristic fit. His precious laptop was cocked on
its side next to the table, open but dark. Broken?

Blinking at the mess, Jaya told herself to back out. Men
in a temper could be dangerous. She knew that.

But there was something so distraught in his body language, in the air even. She immediately hurt for him and
she didn't know why.

"Did something happen?" she queried with subdued
shock.

"Jaya?" His feet rose in surprise. At the same time he
lifted his arm off his eyes. "Did I call you?" Spinning his
feet to the floor in a startling snap to attention, he picked

up his phone and thumbed across the screen. "I was trying not to."

The apology sounded odd, but sometimes English phras-
ing sounded funny to her, with its foreign syntax and slang.
How could you *try not* to call someone?

"I don't mind finding whatever paperwork you need,"
she murmured, compelled to rescue the laptop and hearing
the door pull itself closed behind her. "Especially if you're
dismayed about the way something was handled."

"*Dismayed.* Yeah, that's what I am." He pressed his
mouth flat for a moment, elbows braced on his wide-spread
thighs. His focus moved through her to a place far in the
distance. With a little shudder, he skimmed his hands up
to ruffle his hair before staring at her with heartrending
bleakness. "You've caught me at a bad time."

For some reason her mouth went dry. She didn't react to
men, especially the dark, powerfully built, good-looking
ones. Theo was all of those things, his complexion not as
dark as her countrymen, but he had Greek swarthiness and
dark brown hair and brows. With his short hair on end, he
looked younger than his near thirty. For a second, he reminded her of the poorest children in India, the ones old
enough to have lost hope.

Her hand twitched to smooth his disheveled hair, in-
stinctively aware he wouldn't like anyone seeing him at
less than his most buttoned-down.

He was still incredible. His stubbled jaw was just wide
enough to evenly frame his gravely drawn mouth while his
cheekbones stood out in a way that hollowed his cheeks.
His brows were winged, not too thick, lending a striking
intelligence to his keen brown eyes.

They seemed to expand as she looked into them. The
world around her receded....

"We'll do this tomorrow. Now's not a good time." The

quiet words carried a husky edge that caused a shiver of something visceral to brush over her.

She didn't understand her reaction, certainly didn't know why she was unable to stop staring into his eyes even when a flush of heat washed through her.

"I can't take advantage of your work ethic," he added. "It could undermine our employer-employee relationship."

Appalled, she jerked her gaze to the floor, blushing anew as she processed that she'd been in the throes of a moment and hadn't even properly recognized it as one until her mooning became so obvious he had to shut her down.

How? In the past few years, any sort of sexual aggression on a man's part had stopped her heart. Terror was her reaction and escape her primary instinct. Wistful thoughts like, *I wonder how his stubble would feel against my lips,* had never happened to her, but for a few seconds she'd gone completely dreamy.

Her body flamed like it was on fire, but not only from mortification. There was something else, a curiosity she barely remembered from a million years ago when she'd been a girl talking to a nice boy at school.

If she had the smarts she always claimed to, she'd let his remark stand. She'd excuse herself to Marseille and never be seen again.

At the same time, as discomfited as she was, her ability to have a moment was so heartening she couldn't help standing in place like someone testing cold waters, trying to decide whether to wade farther in.

Not that she'd come here for that. No, she wanted to say goodbye and he'd given her an opening.

"Actually, we don't have that kind of relationship anymore." With jerky movements she set his laptop on the coffee table and pressed the lid closed. "Today was my last day. I should have changed, but I'm having trouble letting go."

He sat back, hands on his knees, taken aback. "Why

wasn't I informed? If you're moving to the competition, we'll match whatever they're offering."

"That's not it." She sank onto the seat opposite him and grasped her hands together so she could portray more composure than she actually possessed. Emotions rose as she realized this was it, no more uniform, no more career with the Makricosta hotel chain, no more Theo. Her voice grew husky. "You—I—I mean the company—have been so good with training me and offering certifications. I would never throw that in your face and run to the competition."

"We believe in investing in our employees."

"I know, but I never dreamed I could go from chambermaid to the front desk in that kind of time, let alone manage the department." She remembered how frightened she'd been of getting in trouble for leaving her cleaning duties when she'd brought a lost little boy to the office, hovering to translate until his parents were located. Theo happened to be conducting one of his audits and was impressed by her mastery of four languages and ability to keep a little one calm.

"My confidence was at a low when I began working here," she confessed with a tough smile. "If you hadn't asked me if I planned to apply for the night clerk job I wouldn't have thought I'd even be considered. I'm really grateful you did that."

There. She'd said what she had wanted to say.

"My sister would disown me if I turned into a sexist," he dismissed, but his gaze went to his phone. His despondency returned to hover in the room like a cloud off dry ice. She sensed that whatever news was affecting him, Adara Makricosta had delivered it.

"Where are you going, if not two doors down?" he asked abruptly.

She lifted her gaze off the strong hands massaging his knees. He wasn't as collected as he was trying to appear.

For some reason, she wanted to take those hands and hold them still and say, *It'll be okay. You'd be surprised what a person can endure.*

"France," she replied, not wanting to talk about her situation, especially when it appeared he was only looking for distraction from his own troubles. "Marseille. It's a family thing. Very sudden. I'm sorry." She wasn't sure why she tacked on the apology. Habits of a woman, she supposed, but she *was* sorry. Sorry that she had to leave this job, sorry she was inconveniencing him, sorry that her cousin was dying.

She felt her mouth pulling down at the corners and ducked her head.

"You're not getting married, are you? This isn't one of those arranged things?" He sounded so aghast she had to smile. Westerners could be so judgmental, like all *his* relationships were love matches rather than practical arrangements.

"No." She lifted her head and he snagged her into another moment.

It occurred to her why she didn't feel threatened by this. They'd had a million of these brief engagements, all very short-lived. For over four years, she'd been glancing up to catch him watching her and he had been looking back to his work so smoothly she had put the charged seconds down to her imagination, convincing herself he didn't even know she was alive.

Our employer-employee relationship...

Was that what had kept him from showing interest before? It wouldn't surprise her. He held himself to very high standards, never making a false move.

But if that was what had held him back, what did it mean for her right now, when she was alone with him in this suite and he knew she was no longer off limits?

Ingrained caution had her measuring the distance to the door, then flicking a reading glance at him.

The air of masculine interest surrounding him fell away and her boss returned. "This is a blow to the company. I'll provide you a reference, of course, but would a leave of absence be more appropriate? Should we keep your job open for you?"

His sudden switch gave her tense nerves a twang, leaving her unsettled. Men never seemed to get her messages to back off. Having Theo read her so clearly was disturbing.

"I—No." She shook her head, trying to stay on topic, tempted to say she'd return, but Saranya's cancer made it very unlikely. She hated to even think about it, but she'd been through it with Human Resources and had to get used to reality. "I'm moving in with my cousin and her husband. She's very ill, won't survive. I'm close with their daughter and she'll need me."

"I'm sorry. That's rough."

She absorbed the quiet platitude with a nod.

"I don't mean to sound crass, but would money help?" he added.

"Thank you, but that's not the issue. My cousin's husband is very well-off. They were extremely good to me when I left India, taking me in until I was able to support myself. I couldn't live with myself if I wasn't with them through this."

"I understand."

Did he? His family seemed so odd. Estranged almost. His remark about his sister a few minutes ago was as personal as she'd ever heard him speak of her. The few occasions when she'd seen any of them together, none had shown warmth or connection.

Who was she to judge, she thought with a jagged pain? She'd been disowned by her family.

He seemed to have equally dismal thoughts. His gaze

dropped to the papers still scattered across the floor. He picked up his drink, but only let it hang in his loose fingers.

"Do you want to talk about…whatever is troubling you?" she asked.

"I'd rather drink myself unconscious." He sipped and scowled, "But I only have watered down soda, so…" He set it aside and stood, giving her the signal that heart-to-heart confessions were off the table.

She tried not to take it as a slight. He was a private man. This was the most revealing she'd ever seen him.

"I'm sorry we won't be working together any longer, Jaya. Our loss is the hoteliers in Marseille's gain. Please contact me if you're interested in working for Makricosta's again. We have three in France."

"I know. Thank you, I will." She swallowed and wondered if she would turn into a complete fool and start to cry. Standing, she put her hand in his and tried for one firm pump with a clean release.

He kept her hand in his warm one. His thumb grazed over the backs of her knuckles.

Her skin tingled and her stomach took a roller coaster dip and swoop.

She looked at his eyes, but he was looking at their hands. Her fingers quivered in his grip as he turned her palm up. She almost thought he was going to raise it to his lips. He looked up and the swooning dip hit harder. That was a *sex* look.

But it was Theo's eyes, Theo's expression that was always so aloof but now glowed with admiration and something else that was aggressive and hungry. He skimmed his gaze down her cheek to her mouth and sensations like fireworks burst through her. Zinging streaks of heat shot down her limbs and detonated her heart into expansive pumps.

She was experiencing sexual excitement, she interpreted

dazedly, and the sensations grew as he stepped closer and lowered his head. He was going to kiss her!

She stiffened with apprehension and he straightened. Her hand wound up hanging in the air ungrasped as he pulled in a strained breath from the ceiling. "You're right. It's not appropriate." Weary despair returned like a cloak to weigh down his shoulders. "I apologize."

"No, I—" *Please* let her dark skin disguise some of these fervent blushes. "You surprised me. I came in here reminding myself not to call you Theo. I didn't think you thought about me like that. I would—" Was she really going to risk this? She had to. She'd never get another chance. "I'd like it if you kissed me."

CHAPTER TWO

"Jaya—"

The gentle let-down in his tone made her cringe. She'd lost him to her habitual rejection of male closeness, but wanting a man to touch her was so *new*. She couldn't help that it scared her.

He searched her face with his gaze. "You have to know how pretty you are. Of course I've noticed you. I've also noticed you don't party like the rest of your age group. You're not the one-night stand type."

"I said a kiss, not that I wanted to sleep with you."

Her swift disdain amused him. He quirked his mouth and tilted back his head. "So you did. You can see what a philanderer I am, it didn't occur to me you weren't offering to stay the night." He made a noise of disparagement that seemed self-directed. His wide shoulders sank another notch.

He appeared so tired and in need of comfort. Conflict held her there another minute. She wanted him to see her as available, yet wanted to self-protect. It was frustrating.

"What age group?" she challenged, pushing herself as much as him. "I'm twenty-five. What are you? Thirty?"

"Are you? You look younger." His mouth twitched again as he reassessed her in a way that incited more contradictory feelings all through her.

Just go, her timid self said. *It's safer.* Her more deeply buried self, the girl who had grown up determined to make something of herself, believing in things like equal rights and reaching her own potential, stood there and tried to make him see her as someone who shouldn't be dismissed. Someone with value and values.

"Having a career is important to me. Makricosta's has been a second chance to build one and I haven't wanted to do anything to jeopardize it. You won't be surprised to hear I send money to my parents. I can't afford to drop shifts because I'm hung-over."

"I'm not surprised at all. You've always struck me as very loyal. And sweet. Virginal even." It was almost a question.

The backs of her eyes stung and she lowered her gaze to her clenched hands. "I'm not," she admitted in a small voice, not wanting those memories to intrude when she felt so safe with him.

"And you've been judged for that? Men and their double standards. I hate my sex. Judge *me*. I sleep with women and never talk to them again. I really do that, Jaya," he confessed with dark self-disgust.

She heard the warning behind his odd attempt to reassure. She appreciated the effort—even though he had it all wrong. Yes, she had been judged, but for a man's crime against her, not any she'd committed.

"I hate men, too," she admitted. *But not you,* she silently added.

"Ah, some bastard broke your heart. I excel at being the rebound guy, you know." Here was the generous tycoon with the hospitable expression who asked a guest if she was enjoying her stay and wound up sharing her table along with further amenities.

"Is that why you pick up those tourists?" she couldn't help teasing, amused by this side of him in spite of her exasperation. "You're offering first aid?"

"I'm a regular paramedic. 'He cheated? He's a fool.'" He shook his head in self-deprecation. "I should be shot."

"Are you really that shallow?" She didn't believe it. The women were always relaxed and euphoric, never morose, when they checked out. She was envious of that. Curious.

"I'm not very deep." He rubbed his face. "But I don't lie. They know what they're getting."

"One night," she clarified, wondering why he thought he had nothing to offer a woman beyond that.

"One night," he agreed with an impactful look. His hands went into his pockets and he rocked back on his heels, saying, "And apparently you restrict to one kiss. But I'll take it if you're still offering."

The craving in his gaze was so naked, she blushed hard enough her cheeks stung. Covering them, she laughed at herself and couldn't meet his eyes. "I'm not a certified attendant."

"There's not a woman in the world with enough training to fix me. Don't try." Another warning, his tone a little cooler.

She shook her head. This was about fixing herself, not him. "I just keep thinking that if I leave without kissing you, I'll always wonder what it would have been like."

That sounded too ingenuous, too needy, but his quietly loaded, "Yeah," seemed to put them on the same page, which was remarkable. He stared at her mouth and hot tingles made her lips feel plump. She tried to lick the sensation away.

His breath rushed out in a ragged exhale. He loomed closer, so tall and broad, blocking out her vision, nearly overwhelming her. But when his fingers lightly caressed her jaw and his mouth came down, she was paralyzed with anticipation.

There'd been a few kisses in her life, none very memorable, but when his mouth settled on hers, unhurried and hot, she knew she'd remember this for the rest of her life.

The smooth texture of his lips sealed to hers. He didn't force her mouth open. She softened and welcomed his confident possession, weakening despite the nervous flutters accosting her. He rocked the fit, deepening the kiss so she opened her mouth wider, bathed in delicious waves of heat. Their lips dampened and slid erotically. His tongue was almost there, then not, then—

He licked into her mouth and she moaned, lashed with exquisite delight. This was the kind of kiss she'd only read about and now she knew there was a reason they called it a soul kiss. Her hand went to his shoulder for balance. She lifted on her toes, wanting more pressure, more of him settling into her inner being.

With a groan, he slid his arm around her and pulled her tight against him, softly crushing her mouth while digging his fingers into her bound hair. It was good, so good. She reached her arms around his neck, loving how it felt to be kissed and held so tightly against his hard chest and—

He was hard *everywhere.*

Like hitting a wall, she pushed back, perturbed by how intensely she had been responding and the dicey situation she'd put herself in.

He didn't let her go right away, kind of steadied her first while staggering one step himself, then he ran a hand through his hair and swore under his breath. "Hellfire, Jaya. I suspected it'd be good, but I didn't know it'd be *that* good. Are you sure you don't want to spend the night?"

"I—" Say no. *Go.* But what if he was the one? The man who would get her past the hurdle of burying her sexuality out of fear? "I really wasn't expecting this." *Liar,* an inner vixen accused. "You're right that I don't have affairs. I don't know if that's what I want right now, but…" She found herself wringing her hands like the virgin he'd accused her of being. "I really liked kissing you."

"Are you trying to let me down gently? Because it's not necessary."

"No! I'm genuinely confused about what I want." It was almost a wail of agony she was so frustrated with herself.

His mouth pulled up on one side in a half grin that might have been patronizing if he hadn't softened it by saying, "You're not the one-night stand type, but your life has been derailed and sex would take your mind off things. Believe me, I sympathize."

She cocked her head, intrigued by these glimpses into the man behind the aloof mask. "Is that why you're asking me to stay?"

"That obvious, am I?"

"You're making me worry for my friends. Is there a problem with Makricosta's?" she probed.

"No," he assured promptly, then sighed and scratched at his hair like he could erase whatever was going on inside his skull. "Mine is a personal derailment. A family thing, not an illness like yours. I've been angry with someone for a very long time and learned today that I have no reason to be. I'm running out of people to hate and blame. I don't know what to do about that."

Kiss me, she thought. She couldn't believe he was opening up to her like this and way in the back of her mind, she suspected he would regret it, but right now it softened her into wanting to heal him. Madness. She was more broken than he was.

"You told me not to try fixing you," she reminded gently. "It's good advice. I honestly don't know if I can be what you're looking for tonight." She wanted to be, but the thought of that kind of intimacy opened such a gaping vulnerability in her, she could hardly breathe. "I keep telling myself to leave." She gestured toward the door.

"But you're still here."

She lifted a shoulder. "It sends the wrong message, I know."

Their gazes tangled and all she could think about was the heart-racing kiss they'd just shared. He claimed he was the opposite of a gentleman, but she sensed that despite his rock-hard physical power and authoritative command, he was capable of gentleness.

"Give up on me at any point. It won't bother me a bit," he coaxed with surface nonchalance, but she sensed a tighter intensity beneath. Because he wanted her that badly? Or the mental escape?

"Really?" She folded her arms, highly skeptical.

"It's a lady's prerogative to change her mind," he said with a fatalistic shrug, then grinned with surprising wickedness. "But I'll do my best to keep it interesting."

Her equilibrium rolled and dipped again, making her unsteady on her feet.

"I can't believe I'm having this conversation," she said, shaking her head at her own waffling forwardness and his sexual arrogance. "With *you*."

"I've trained myself not to fantasize about women wearing that uniform. It's pretty surreal for me, too."

She chuckled, then sobered as she met his avid look. He was holding himself under tight control and she suspected she'd always been aware of his ruthless self-discipline, that it was one of his qualities she was most attracted to.

"I really can't decide, Theo."

His expression eased a little. "You don't have to." He snagged her hand and led her to the sofa, his manner laconic. "We'll take it one kiss at a time. See how it goes."

"You *really* want to take your mind off things."

"I really do," he admitted, dropping onto the sofa and bringing her down beside him. "Will you take your hair down for me?"

After a tiny hesitation, she did, feeling incredibly vulnerable, like she was removing her clothing. Her severe appearance was a shield. Freeing her hair invited him to stroke his fingers through it. He fanned it out from her ear, creating tickling sensations in her scalp as he marveled at the length.

"It's so silky," he murmured.

No product or bleach to make it brittle, she almost said, then decided this would go better if she didn't compare herself to other women whose hair he had petted.

His patience surprised her. She didn't know why, seeing as he was the most unflappable man she'd ever met, but his contentment to take his time combing her hair with his fingers when he seemed so intent on getting physical almost made her worry he was changing his mind. Just when she grew restless, however, he flicked the tie at her throat.

"Can we take this off?" He tugged to loosen the bow.

"Are you going to tie me up with it?" she asked, trying to sound light, but filled with trepidation.

"Do you want me to?" His gaze skimmed over her as though he was reassessing all his preconceptions about her.

"No." Firm. Prudish even.

His lips twitched, but when his gaze came up from watching the scarf trail down her lapel, his lids were heavy and his voice laconic. "Good, because I want to feel your hands on me."

The scarf floated away and he moved in, settling a lazy, drawn-out kiss on her mouth that was reassuringly tender and sweet.

And, after a while, a tiny bit frustrating. She wanted more than this slow pace. She wanted the hand climbing her waist to quit stopping at the underside of her breast. *Touch me,* she willed, breasts feeling swollen and achy. She wanted the space where they leaned into each other to close so she could press herself to his wide chest. He'd come out of the private lap pool here once, when she'd arrived with a file. Even though he'd shrugged on a shirt immediately, his washboard abs had been full-on. He was gorgeous and she wanted to see his naked chest again.

She plucked at the buttons on his shirt, not quite nervy enough to tug them open.

He broke away to look down at where her indecisive fingers lifted away from his breastbone. Without a word, he one-handedly yanked, disregarding the exceptional quality by tearing its holes, pulling it free of his waistband at the same time so it hung loose on his shoulders.

Gasping at his near savagery, she touched her fingertips to her sensitized lips.

He caught her hand and bit softly against the plump pad at the base of her thumb. "I'm dying for you to touch me. Don't worry, I won't rip your uniform. We'd have to account for the loss."

His husky comment made her laugh. Half of her dry chuckle was mild terror because he was taking her hand to his chest. She caught her breath as her fingerprints made contact with the heat of his skin, taut over his hard muscles.

He shivered under her touch.

"You're so hot," she murmured.

"Thank you. I've always thought the same about you."

Smiling, she did something she hadn't imagined she could. She leaned in and kissed his mouth while both her hands skimmed over the intriguing ripples of his upper chest, exploring the texture of a light sprinkle of hair and satin skin over muscles that flexed under her caress.

He groaned, but rather than gather her into a tight crush, she felt a tickling graze of fingers between her breasts. A second later, she was the one to draw back and watch as he finished opening her white-and-red Makricosta blouse.

Her ivory bra beneath was practical and almost adolescent. She didn't have much to support and had never seen the point in spending money on something only she would see. An urge to apologize rose to the back of her throat, but the way he traced the top of one small cup, caressing the upper slope of her breast, had her holding her breath.

"I have a wicked addiction to cocoa," he told her as he took his time spreading the shirt wide on her shoulders, patiently tugging it free of her skirt. His returning touch was whisper-soft as he grazed her ribs and found his way to the clasp in the middle of her back.

Her back arched from his caress and her bra loosened. She drew in a breath, hesitant, but his hand came around and cupped her breast. The sensation blanked her mind, holding her in thrall. So much heat. He was like an inferno, and so masculine, but reverent. There was aggression, she could feel the possessiveness in the way he enclosed her like he had every right, his touch firm, but he was gentle at the same time. Softly crushing, as if he knew she would enjoy the sensation of pressure increasing by degrees. He massaged flesh that felt heavy and achy and prickling in one tight spot.

His touch shifted as he leaned in to capture her mouth. Muscle flexed under her hands as she met his searching kiss with welcome. Sensations overwhelmed her, but a particularly sharp one pierced through her psyche. He thumbed her nipple, making it feel knotted and tighter and more sensitive. And so vulnerable, yet excited.

She whimpered, distressed by the rocketing spikes of pleasure going straight through her abdomen into a place that had retreated to hibernation a long time ago.

"God, Jaya, let me taste you."

He pressed her onto her back on the cushions, covering her so smoothly she didn't realize how she'd wound up under him, her bra pushed up and his weight pinning her hips, one leg between his, the other dangling off the edge of the cushions.

A gasp of shock scraped her throat as she pulled in air, trying to catch up to this new circumstance, trying to decide if she was okay with it.

"So gorgeous."

Damp heat closed over the pulsing tip of her breast. Knifing spears of delight pulled upward from her flesh.

Be scared, she told herself, but the scariest thing was how devastating this pleasure was. Her hands couldn't get enough of roaming his back. His bunched shirt kept getting in the way, irritating her. His weight on her should have terrified her, but when she bucked, it was slowly, because she couldn't help herself. Her leg couldn't find purchase alongside his so she let her ankle curl behind his thigh.

And she moaned. Aloud. Even though a distant voice said, *Don't. Don't be sexual, don't encourage him, don't embarrass yourself.* She couldn't help it. He had both her breasts cupped into mounds that he sipped and licked and tortured. It was incredible.

"Theo, I can't stand it."

He lifted to kiss her, swooping like a predator to ravage her mouth as he shifted their position and was fully between her legs. The layers of her wrinkled skirt had climbed so his fly came into firm contact with the cotton of her underpants.

Panic began to edge out her arousal.

She pressed his shoulders and he broke their kiss to set his damp forehead against hers. "I know, I'm pushing it, but this is as far as we're going. I've just realized I don't have any condoms." He smoothed her hair back from what must have been a stunned expression and kissed her once, quite hard. "You have no idea how sorry I am."

She did. Her hips wriggled involuntarily and he shuddered, pressing that most assertive part of himself to her vulnerable softness, pinning her motionless as he released a dry laugh.

"Okay, maybe you do." Kissing her with regret, he grazed his lips over her cheekbones and eyebrow. "You feel so good. You're so pretty. I don't want to stop touching you." His hand skimmed the outside of her thigh, making her trembling muscles contract to tighten her leg against him. "Will you let me make it good for you, at least? Can I know what it feels like to touch you?"

He set a sweet kiss on her chin while his hand climbed under her gathered skirt and learned the style and texture of her mood-killing matronly underpants.

She opened her mouth, thoughts scattering in a dozen directions by arousal and conflicting misgivings. Her mind refused to fix on anything let alone a clear yes or no.

Before she could form words, he shifted enough to cover her mound with a compelling rock of his hand. Stars shot behind the backs of her eyes.

"Like that?" he murmured, licking her neck and easing his touch to a lighter caress through the layer of cotton. Just a soft trace against a very intimate place that made her pulse with need. "Softer? Tell me what you like."

"I didn't come here for this," she managed to whisper, aware that she was becoming completely abandoned, letting her legs fall open to his incredible facility with a woman's body. Wanting whatever he'd give her. "But it feels so good."

"I know. Hate me later, but right now can I keep doing this? You're so incredible…"

He kissed her neck and sidled his touch beneath the cotton, knowing exactly what he was doing in a way that should have alarmed her, but she didn't care. At this moment, she really didn't care about anything except that he keep his attention on that exquisite bunch of nerves tangled into a signal that sent ripples outward through her abdomen. He wasn't in any hurry, seeming to luxuriate in circling and stroking, driving her crazy.

She bit at his lips, dying, wild, loving his touch and him for giving her this amazing build of pleasure, this incessant desire for physical contact with a man.

He said sinful things about what he wanted to do to her, sucked her nipple and said, "Let me kiss you here. I want to lick you. It'll be so good, Jaya—"

"No," she gasped. Her horror was pure, latent shyness, but the idea of him doing that was so wickedly intriguing her arousal spiked to something she couldn't contain. Convulsively trying to close her legs, she could only squeeze his wide, masculine hips, unable to stop what he was doing. She couldn't catch back her uninhibited response. Her only choice was complete surrender to him and her body's sharp need.

Her reward was a deep throb of sheer joy expanding through her in shuddering waves. Her throat filled with a cry of release that was more than just physical. It was emotional triumph. Freedom from the past. Joy at a man's touch.

CHAPTER THREE

INCREDIBLE TENDERNESS MADE her slither in sweet lassitude beneath him, loving the hard strength of him, the disheveled intensity holding him tense as she ran her fingers into his hair. She made him lift his head so she could look at him.

It was painfully intimate to let him look into her eyes when she had just shattered so completely. His hand stilled where he still had it tucked against her mons and an internal ache made her long to beg him to continue stroking her.

"Thank you," she whispered, hoping he put down her shiny eyes to arousal.

A slow, wicked grin spread across his face. "Stick around. There's more where that came from." He punctuated with a gentle, deliberate caress that slid low and penetrated her pulsing channel.

She tightened, part of her reaction instinctual resistance, but the sensation of clasping his thick finger was so delicious she moaned and lifted her hips a little, encouraging more.

"Ah, Jaya…" His hot mouth opened in a wet kiss against her neck and he deepened his possession of her.

"Wait," she gasped, still clasping his head and this time clutching him close with her arms hard on his shoulders while she stared at the back of the sofa. Was she really going to do this? Her body was on fire while her mind was cleaving in all directions.

He removed his hand from her underpants and she moaned in loss.

"It's okay," he murmured, skimming his lips against her jaw before he lifted his head and removed her hand from his hair. "You don't have to rip my hair out. This has gone further than you wanted to, I get it."

"No, I—" Disconcerted, she dropped her twitching fingers to his shoulders, sorry she'd hurt him, sorry she'd lost his exquisite caresses. She didn't want this to end, not yet. This was her chance to get over her past. "I have a pill in my room. One that, um, prevents a pregnancy after, um, unprotected sex." *Please don't ask me why I have it.*

Her voice faded toward the end. She was grossly unsure of herself and given how he'd pulled away, maybe he wasn't all that invested. He became very grave as he pondered what she'd said, making her hold her breath.

"I always wear a condom."

Disappointment sliced surprisingly deep. She swallowed and nodded. "I understand. It's okay. Like you said, this isn't something we intended, so—"

"No, I mean I'm clean. I've never gone bareback so you don't have to worry I'd give you anything."

"I…" *Had tests.* Again, she didn't want to think about Saranya taking her to the doctor once she'd got her out of India. That dark time was being overcome, here, tonight, with this man. "I'm clean, too."

He searched her face. She recognized the glaze of concentration in his eyes as a passionate force. It nearly squeezed the air right out of her.

"Swear to me you'll take that pill." His lips barely moved.

"My family would take out a contract on me if I had a baby outside of marriage."

He held himself in steely control and she could almost hear the computations of risk against desire. "I don't want to be a father. Ever. If you're thinking this might lead to something—"

"No!" she insisted, casting for the right words. "It's like you said about not wanting to think about certain things. I want something different in my mind." *A new memory. A good one.* "A baby would be a disaster. But I want to feel... you," she ended in a whisper.

His nostrils flared as he drew a deep breath, his nod brief and sharp before he pulled away, gathering her up as he found his feet. The strength in him as he lifted her and held her cradled to his chest made bells ring in her ears, but she found herself curling her arm around his neck and burying her face into the masculine scent in the crook near his shoulder.

What she had said was broad enough to be true in many ways. She wanted to think of men differently, but there was a part of her deeply enthralled in the now. She could barely form a thought beyond her need for physical contact with this man.

He set her on the bed and straightened, not turning on the light. Only the faint glimmer from the pool deck through the windows penetrated.

She hugged her knees as she watched him slide his belt free and toss it away, toeing off his shoes at the same time.

"Are we taking turns? Because I'm dying to see you," he said with enough ragged edge on his voice to make her shiver.

She looked down at her crumpled uniform, her shirt open, her bra still loose across her chest. Shyness was the only thing holding her back from undressing, she realized with a glistening lilt of joy. Not fear, just natural self-consciousness about undressing in front of a man.

As she hesitantly drew her shirt off her shoulders she confessed, "You've seen a lot of women. I don't know how I'll compare."

Down to his briefs as he peeled away his socks, he said, "I'm not very sure of my ability to hang on until I've given you everything I want you to have. I do *not* want to be the selfish bastard you compare every future lover to."

He wouldn't be, not by a long shot. And even though a quick coupling was probably better for her, given her hang-ups, she doubted it was a good thing to say. Besides, he stole the shirt she was trying to fold and lifted her bra away, dropping both to the floor. The air-conditioned room made her curl her toes, incredibly self-conscious of her naked breasts and beaded nipples as she forced her hands to remain beside her hips.

Sitting there in the half-light, staring at his muscled frame, she was accosted by a pull in her abdomen, but it wasn't fear or misgivings. It was longing. She wanted his hot, muscled body on hers. She wanted to feel those hard thighs between her own without cloth between them.

He started to remove her sandals and she kicked them off herself, letting him ease her onto her back in a sprawl under him as he loomed over her. The brush of his skin against hers was brand-hot, making her quiver with disconcertion. But the reassuring stroke of his hand up her waist to cup her breast calmed her nerves even as his expert touch sensitized her.

"Did I mention my addiction to cocoa?" he asked huskily. "I could sip these chocolate nipples of yours all night."

He bent to enclose her in wet heat and the return of excitement was like a blow, bringing up one of her knees. Sweet delight flashed through her, rippling waves of pleasure that didn't fade, only increased.

"I want to kiss you," she admitted as he shifted to tease her other breast. A coiled knot of tension pulled in her abdomen. It made her bold, impatient for the build and release of orgasm.

As he lifted his head to look at her, he skimmed a hand

down, silently asking her to lift her hips so he could push her skirt off. When had he lowered the zipper?

She complied and he reared up onto his knees, stealing the last of her clothes. Her thighs twitched, locking closed in nervous tension while she stared at the black briefs hugged tight to his hips and thighs. His erection was a thick, unapologetic ridge behind the stretchy fabric.

He sat back on his heels, knees splayed, hands in loose fists against his thighs. He let out a harsh breath, like he was under strain. "God, you're pretty."

He says it to all of them, she warned herself, but she couldn't help smiling. The way he studied her with the intensity he usually reserved for spreadsheets, but had that light of excitement and wolfish half smile on his face, seemed like genuine admiration. It affected her, relaxing her and making her want to writhe invitingly—if only she knew how.

"Will you kiss me again? Please?" She lifted a hand and he let out a gruff laugh as he stretched out beside her, leaning over her.

"I'll kiss every inch of you." He gathered her up to his muscled body and she felt bruised by the hardness of him. He was so hot, so strong beneath his taut, satiny skin. She couldn't resist stroking his back and shoulders as he kissed her. Their tongues flicked and delved and it felt totally natural. Better than natural. Necessary.

She did writhe then, moved by instinct, body involuntarily lifting into the stroke of his hands, arching to push her breast into his cupped palm, rolling her face into his caressing fingertips when he dragged his mouth to her neck. Then he was laving her nipple again, bringing the ferocious need into her loins. Mother Nature had a plan, quite obviously. She ached for attention between her thighs.

If only she knew how to make love as well as he did. He massaged her belly and grazed fingertips along the seam of her thighs, inciting her to relax them open. Then, finally, he was tracing into her wet heat, penetrating easily into the dampness that welcomed him. His caress was so stunningly *good.* As his thumb rolled over the taut peak of her clitoris, tiny sparks shimmered through her, gathering toward the implosion. She gasped, awed that she could feel this way again, from this deeply intimate touch.

He shifted, licked under her breast and kissed a trail down her abdomen.

"Theo," she panted.

"Every inch, Jaya." He left off caressing her and used his damp hand to crook her knee open, pressing a firm kiss to her inner thigh.

"No, Theo, please don't."

"Don't be shy." He came back onto his elbow beside her, his expression so feral and aroused she ought to have been terrified, but his voice was calm and controlled, his hand on her navel soothing. "I am seriously worried about not being able to last once I get my skivvies off. Let me make it good for you."

While a nervous giggle bubbled in her at his blunt remark, she knew her limits.

"This *is* good for me." Her voice hitched with deep emotion and she glanced up through stinging eyes, hoping he couldn't see in the shadowed light how out of sorts she was—enthralled and uneasy, but resolved. "I want to feel you inside me."

He muttered a curse, closing his eyes and averting his face.

Pressing into the mattress, she asked warily, "Are you angry?"

"What? No. But you're not helping my control with talk like that. Do you have any idea how long I've wanted to be inside you? Years. Since the first time I saw you."

He jackknifed off the bed, giving her space as he continued his grumbling tirade while stripping his briefs.

"You said earlier that you didn't know I thought about you this way. Well, you've never once hinted you did, either. Do you know how sexy it is to hear you want me?"

As he straightened, she thought, *"want" is debatable.* She wanted to feel normal. She wanted to feel close to Theo. But that aggressive thrust of masculine power made her apprehensive.

He came back to cover her, a practiced knee pressing her legs open as he settled on her. She stiffened, waiting for the breach, but he only cupped her face and set a soft kiss on her upper lip.

"Did I kill the mood? I didn't mean to. This is the most bizarre night of my life."

"That sort of flattery restores it," she teased, because this was the considerate Theo she recognized. Even so, she was hyperaware of the hard, thick muscle pressed so close to her vulnerable folds.

Rather than laugh, he released a sigh that was hot and damp against her cheek. "I'm grateful you're here, Jaya. All the crap outside these walls…It can't touch us right now. I hope you feel like that, too. I don't want to be the only one finding escape."

"You're not," she assured him, shivering in nervousness, but certain this was what she wanted: escape from her past. "I'm using you, too."

"Good." He kissed her, the familiar press and pull drawing her back toward the arousal that had been simmering under her last-minute nerves. When he rocked his hips he furrowed open the softness of her, finding and reawakening her to pleasure, she jerked, surprised by the spike of desire.

His big body overwhelmed hers, but there was a sense of safety here, too. His chest rubbed hers, stimulating her nipples. His thighs were tense and abrasive, but she couldn't help stroking his legs with hers, oddly entranced by the sensation, inadvertently parting her legs and opening herself with the movement.

Her undulations brought him to her entrance. A whimper of mixed emotion escaped her, but she cradled his head and stroked the back of his neck and lifted her hips into the pressure, making this happen.

She braced for pain, but there was only a tremendous sense of fullness as he slid into her. Her muscles tightened instinctually, but that only heightened the friction— the sweet, delicious friction—of his burying himself deep into her body.

A shudder of reaction took her.

He squeezed her in constrictor arms, rocking himself deep and tight against her body, sending glittering sensations through her as he whispered, "Already? That's okay, I'm really close, too. Come for me. Let me feel it."

She caught back a sob, not hurt, not ready to orgasm, but shattered emotionally by how complete she felt. Pride in herself almost burst her apart, making her cling to him, wanting this moment of perfection to imprint in her mind forever.

After a few seconds, when she only stayed very still beneath him, he murmured, "Together then?" against her temple. His hard arms caged her as he withdrew and returned. "Tell me when."

Pure white light seemed to expand in her as he fit himself to her depths.

"Oh, Theo."

"Yeah." He thrust again, deeper. Like he wanted to lock himself into her forever.

It was fantastic. Sweet and primal and delicious.

And not enough.

"Don't stop," she gasped.

"Never." He kept moving, his hips meeting hers with more force.

Sensations danced with giddy promise through her. She couldn't speak, could only brace for another pulse as he returned again, his muscled tension a gathered force over and around her. Like a storm building.

She panted, greeting each thrust with an arching welcome of her hips. Thought receded and she embraced pure womanhood, primitive and earthy and natural as they mated. His scent was perfume, his groans behind his gritted teeth music. She smiled at her power over him and herself, reveling in the dance. Cries built in her throat as the silver threads of crisis gathered. Her hand went to his buttock, nails digging in as she tried to push him deeper, needing just a little more. She was so close.

Sweat adhered them and they struggled in ecstatic perfection, almost there, almost there…

Orgasm ripped through her and her ragged cry was pure liberation. Absolute completion as her body shuddered and clasped at his.

He let out a fierce shout of his own. In her trembling sheathe, his thick shaft pulsed, filling her with volcanic heat. She closed her arms and legs around him and willed this union to last forever.

CHAPTER FOUR

Present day...

AS HE SETTLED onto the tarmac Theo eyed the waiting limo. Jaya was smart enough to wait for the blades to slow before leaving the car, but he was anxious to see her. He told himself it was the babies he was worried about, and whether he'd have the help he needed in caring for them. It had nothing to do with the gnawing ache that had stayed with him during the eighteen months since he'd made love to her for hours before she'd hurriedly dressed so she wouldn't miss her flight.

His gut knotted. She'd seen him with his defenses blown apart by the family strife he'd been trying all his life to wall off. He'd never been as unguarded with a woman as he'd been that night, usually focusing strictly on the physical pleasure of his encounters and saying as little as possible.

With her, he'd reveled in the cessation of emotional pain. When she'd left him to the silence of the suite, he'd blamed his plummet back into misery on the return of his dark memories from childhood, but there was more to it. He used to look forward to Bali; he hated it there now. He missed her.

And he couldn't imagine how she'd react to this. He glanced back to the passenger cabin, able to see through the open door that his nephew had fallen asleep. His niece stared wide-eyed from a tear-stained face, startled into silence by the return to solid ground and the new noises of shutting down the chopper.

"I'll be right back," he told her, not sure if his words had any impact. He dropped outside to tether the machine. He'd fueled here in the past, so the hangar wasn't unknown. He still didn't like leaving his machine without prior arrangements. Choice, however, had been pitched into the Med when he'd flown out to the new Makricosta cruise ship only to see a gunner boat approaching from the horizon.

His brother-in-law, Gideon, had been all smiles on his arrival, bringing the babies to have a look at uncle's helicopter. The second Theo had delivered the news he hadn't wanted to share over the radio, Gideon's hand had bit into his arm. "You have to get them off this ship."

Not only did Theo have no idea what would happen to his sister and older brother, or their spouses, but what in *hell* would he do with two babies? Especially if this turned into a permanent situation?

Forget the worst-case scenarios, he reminded himself. Deal with the moment at hand. By his estimation, he had to perform triage for twelve to twenty-four hours before he'd receive new information that would allow him to make a fresh decision.

The limo driver came around to open the back door. Jaya emerged.

Until he saw her and his tension bled away, he hadn't realized how fearful he'd been that she wouldn't come.

The rotors had slowed to listless circles, but he was still struck by a sensation of wind gusting him off his feet. She was wearing her hair shorter, just long enough to touch her shoulders and it had a wave in it he'd never seen before. He liked it better than the tight, sleek bun. She looked younger and more carefree.

Sexy.

Not to say she wasn't looking professional and confident at the same time. Her suit was tailored and chic, the scarf at her throat familiar. A deliberately distancing touch, he wondered, since it was *not* Makricosta colors?

Are you going to tie me up with it?

Do you want me to?

She'd run her fingers through his hair and he'd almost died. Hell, he'd been so needy it was demoralizing.

She smoothed her hands down her jacket, the navy and ice-yellow smart and flattering on her slender figure. Her big, round sunglasses stayed firmly in place as she waited by the open door of the car, not approaching.

He motioned her to come into the interior of the helicopter. After a brief hesitation, she walked forward.

"Mr. Makricosta—"

He paused with one foot on the step and looked back at her, his ghostly reflection in her lenses a picture of one shielded face confronting another.

"Theo," he corrected, tempted to stand here until she said it, which was inane. If he'd had one plan when—*if* he ever saw her again, it was that he'd pretend they'd never slept together. Unfortunately, he kept hearing her whispery gasps of his name, lightly accented, in his dreams and wanted to know if he remembered it right.

"Would you please tell me what is going on?" A hitch of panic entered her tone as he let her question launch him up the steps and into the helicopter. She followed, protesting, "I can't go anywhere. I have commitments. Work and...."

She didn't finish, making him wonder what other commitments, but he didn't press her. "You got my text. You know I need a room. Somewhere no one will expect me to hole up. When I said this was an emergency—"

He indicated the two babies. He'd had the white leather seats outfitted with child harnesses so he could transport his siblings and their children, but the babies looked ridiculously tiny in the first-class armchairs.

"*You have kids?*" she screeched, standing taller in the low-ceilinged inner lounge of the Eurocopter.

Androu jerked awake and began to wail. Evie broke down into renewed tears.

"Nice going," he shot at Jaya.

She stared at Androu, seeming to go yellow beneath her natural mocha tone. "How old is he?" she hissed.

"They're not mine," he ground out, resisting a weird guilt attack even though he'd taken pains—and it had been painful—to ignore her messages and reinforce to her that she didn't have any claim on him. "Help me get them into the car." He handed her Androu and turned to unstrap Evie.

She took the boy into her arms like a natural, which he'd known she would be, even though her lips were so pale and frozen he wondered if she'd ever smile again.

It wasn't in her to take out her feelings on a child, though. The first time he'd seen her, a blond German boy's pale hand clutched in hers, he'd recognized her strong maternal instinct and liked her for it. Today she soothed Androu as she carried him outside where the change of scenery calmed him.

Evie remained stiff in his arms, inconsolable. They slid into the limo like bank robbers after a heist and the driver pulled away.

"You might have told me so I could have had proper car seats installed. This is dangerous, Theo."

Damn. His name sounded better than he remembered and made him hunger to hear it against his ear.

"So?" she prompted. "Who are they?"

"Can he be trusted?" he asked in a murmur, nodding at the driver. "Because I couldn't risk a phone call that might have been heard over the radio. I was texting one-handed—" He was interrupted by Jaya's sudden query to Evie.

"*Pyaari beti,* do you have to use the potty?"

Evie's distressed face nodded vigorously.

For the second time today, Theo's mind blanked with panic. She was on his knee!

"Oscar—" Jaya turned to say, but the driver was ahead of her, already slowing outside the terminal building.

"Wait—" Theo said as Jaya plunked Androu onto the cushion beside her and scooped up Evie.

"There's no waiting at her age. What is she, two?" She was out the door as the limo halted, the little girl wrapped onto her hip like a monkey.

Theo clenched his teeth and did the math on discover-ability. He didn't dare let himself calculate the odds on Jaya stealing the toddler. He made himself believe he knew her better, even though he didn't. Not really. Not when he'd treated her the way he had.

Sleeping with Jaya had been wrong.

He wasn't a man who got anything wrong. Mistakes were a luxury he had never been able to afford.

Something about Jaya eroded his discipline, however. Two years ago, he'd started allowing himself to fantasize about an employee. Then he'd begun finding reasons to stay an extra day in Bali, to review reports he could gener-ate himself. He'd rationalized a one-night affair and taken her to bed knowing it was not just unwise and bordering on unethical, it was downright stupid. She was sweet and generous, not the worldly, here-for-a-good-time kind of woman who would forget him as quickly as he forgot her.

God, he wished he could forget her.

The best he'd managed was not to return her tentative few calls. It had been a cruel-to-be-kind favor in her best interest. Not that he expected her to see it that way, but he had warned her they had no future. Surely she wouldn't hold a grudge when he'd been honest about that much?

Skipping his gaze between Androu, who was turning himself and scooting backward off the opposite seat, and the terminal doors that remained closed and reflected the black windows of the limo, he evaluated how much of a chance he was taking letting Jaya whisk Evie into public.

This airstrip catered to private aircraft belonging to celebrities and Europe's high society, which meant most people would have very little interest in anyone but themselves. It was a tempting place for paparazzi to hang around looking for the shot of their career, though. Evie's parents were scrupulous about keeping her out of the limelight. Dressed in her hotel uniform, Jaya would be dismissed as a flight attendant or a nanny. Since Evie's almond eyes and black pigtails didn't match either her adoptive father's blond hair or her mother's green eyes, the chances of anyone recognizing her were narrow.

It was still an interminable wait as Androu rocked his still learning feet across the short expanse to clutch at Theo's knee. "Mama," he said.

Oh, hell. Theo stared into innocent eyes that could have belonged to his little brother, Demitri, at that age. "I know, buddy," he said, even though he didn't know a damned thing except that Adara had done this surrogate parenting at a far younger age than he was, so he had to man up and make this work.

Adara had had Jaya's instincts, though. Somehow she'd hung on to them through the war ground that was their childhood and look what she'd made: Androu was a happy little cub who'd eaten fistfuls of his first birthday cake a few months ago.

"Papa," Androu said, making his request in that polite yet firm way his father had.

"Not here, either, sport." Theo eyed the driver who was

circumspectly keeping his eyes forward. *Discreet,* he'd said in his text to Jaya. *Emergency. I need discreet transport and accommodation.* He'd told her where and when to pick him up and she'd come through for him. Surely that meant she'd bring back his niece.

Androu picked at the seam on Theo's jeans, absorbed, allowing Theo to train his X-ray vision on the terminal doors, willing them to open.

What in hell was taking so long? A tiny thing like Evie couldn't have much liquid in her, especially when she'd cried most of it out. Thank goodness he'd had the sense to call Jaya. Putting a little girl on a potty was not something he would think to do, let alone know how to make happen. He was completely unprepared for this situation, like he'd been dropped on a deserted island with two little gremlins.

And Jaya.

God, she looked more incredible than ever. He still dreamed of that mouth, wide and full and feminine. Her body was better than ever. If he wasn't mistaken, she was holding onto a few more pounds, filling out her slender figure to voluptuous perfection. Her breast would probably overflow his hand when—

If.

Hell, *never.*

It couldn't happen. Best to cut those thoughts short now. Seriously, what was she *doing?*

He couldn't go after her, no matter how much he was tempted. He wasn't a movie star, but the Makricosta siblings had been featured in upscale magazines recently, promoting the cruise ship currently being taken over by pirates. Was it targeted? Were high seas criminals after a hefty ransom by kidnapping some of the richest people in the world? The inaugural cruise had drawn a very elite crowd.

One thing at a time, he ordered himself. Gideon would protect Adara at all costs and he, Theo, had removed the only distraction Gideon might have had. Once the tots were safely stationed, he'd check in with Gideon and the authorities Gideon had raced off to advise.

A sharp pain in his thigh had him jerking his knee from the source, jostling the boy who'd bent to taste denim with his newly cut teeth. Startled by his near fall, the corners of Androu's mouth went down and his eyes filled again.

"Wait. It's fine. Go ahead and use me as a chew toy. You just startled me."

Outside, the terminal doors slid open and Jaya appeared with Evie still on her hip. She clutched an overstuffed bag in her free hand and wore a harried look.

Theo moved faster than the driver, pushing open the door as she reached the car.

"Seriously? Shopping?" He took the bag and steadied her under an elbow as she crawled in, catching a full inhale of her exotic sandalwood and almond scent. It hit him like a drug that weakened his muscles and teased him with euphoria.

Unless he was very careful, coming to her would turn into another mistake. He couldn't let it happen. He released her to pull the door shut behind her.

"Funny," Jaya said tartly, then, "Thank you, Oscar. Directly to the hotel now, please. The underground entrance." She pressed a button to close the privacy window and steadied Evie beside her on the seat as the car began to glide forward.

Theo picked up Androu and settled him on his thigh, catching a look on Jaya's face that might have been stunned hurt, but she looked away. Better that she was hurt and hated him. It would be easier for both of them.

Turning a gentle smile to Evie, she said, "You've been very patient. Would you like your drink now?" She brought a bottle of water out of the bag and opened it, helping Evie to sip.

Androu put out a hand and made a noise of imperative.

"I bought one for him, too. Do you know if they have any allergies?"

"I don't think so." Not Androu anyway. Adara was always prattling on about every little thing Androu ate, touched or said. Theo only listened with half an ear, but he would remember if she was worried about something like that.

There were bananas in the bag with yoghurt cups and a bag of vanilla cookies. Food. Right.

"Good call," he told her as he spilled water all over himself trying to keep the greedy Androu from drowning. The kid didn't have the first clue about the physics of tipping a water bottle and ended up coughing it all down his chin. "I think he uses a special cup for this."

"Really? Perhaps you should have stolen it when you kidnapped him." She brought out a banana and broke off pieces, making everyone sticky but quiet and happy.

"This is Androu, my nephew, Adara and Gideon's boy."

"Oh, of course." Everything in Jaya changed, softening as her gaze hooked onto Androu's little face with as much fixation as her first stare, but with a touch of wistfulness now. "I'd heard gossip about a miscarriage when I was in Bali. I'm happy for them. He's beautiful."

Her tone was sincere, moved almost. Or maybe he was reading into it. His emotions had been stripped to their rawest form the last time he'd been with her. Today wasn't much better. He hadn't planned ever to see her again and when he had indulged in imagining he might, he'd pulled himself together.

"It's been an eventful couple of years," he couched, trying to gloss over all the inner tearing down and rebuilding he'd been forced to do without betraying how brutal it had been. "Look, Jaya. I came to you because I figured I could trust you. We've kept some family business out of the papers for my mother's sake and even though she's gone now, we prefer not to air our dirty laundry, but…" He shrugged. "Are you aware that Nic Marcussen is my older brother?"

"No, I didn't even know your mother had died. I'm so sor— Wait. Marcussen Media? *That* Nic Marcussen?"

"Yes."

"Married to Rowan Davidson, the actress? Who adopted a baby from—" She looked at Evie who tilted her almond-shaped eyes up curiously.

"Where's Mama?"

"She's coming to get you soon," Jaya reassured her, handing Evie another piece of banana. "Isn't she?" she prompted Theo.

"I sincerely hope so, but from what I saw from the air, they have to evade pirates first."

"Where? On the Med? You can't be serious!"

"I know what I saw and the authorities have been notified, but there's every chance we'll be looking at ransom negotiations. The last thing we need is a media circus, especially around the babies. Hell, they're kidnap targets. You were the closest person I could think of who could provide me a place to stay that was off the radar."

Completely practical, exactly as it was supposed to be, he assured himself.

"You knew where I was working?" Her clipped challenge held dual notes of hurt and ire, suggesting that if he had known, he should have called.

He bit back a sigh. "I was contacted as a reference," he lied, adding politely, "Congratulations."

"Oh, um, thanks," she dismissed with a self-conscious shrug. "It's a boutique hotel, very well respected even before the upgrades. They're looking to bring in a higher clientele and hired me because of my experience with Makricosta's. I guess I'm indebted to you…again." Her voice trailed off. The way she bit her lips together sug-

gested she would rather be run over by this limo than face
him after referencing their night together.

He pretended they'd left it at the point where she'd
thanked him, as if the rest hadn't happened. "As I said
then, the hoteliers here got lucky."

Her eyelashes flinched in a way that seemed to say, *Did
you really just say that?*

He had. It was unkind, but he wasn't about to acknowledge how lucky he'd been that night. If his insensitivity
toward her made his gut knot with sick self-hatred, so be
it. He was here for only one reason.

Jaya visibly pulled herself together. "I've arranged the
Presidential Suite. It's yours as long as you need it. I'll talk
to the staff, keep housekeeping out of there, tell them you're
antisocial." Her tight smile said, *It's not even a lie,* and the
churning rolled in his stomach again. "My new boss isn't
nearly as hands-on as you were. You'll be long gone before
he asks who was in there."

Hands-on?

Her cool delivery let him know that two could play this
game.

Androu curled his banana-coated fingers into Theo's
shirtfront and tried to wriggle down to his feet, forcing
Theo to break their stare.

"I need more than a safe place to hide," Theo said, tentative in his struggle with Androu, afraid of hurting his tiny
body, but not wanting him hurting himself by trying to
walk around in a moving vehicle. Androu grew frustrated
and started arching with temper. "I don't know what to do
with babies. I need your help."

"Like a nanny? I can call an agen—"

He shook his head, impatient that she was being obtuse.
"I can't trust strangers. That chauffeur hearing my name
is bad enough. I need complete discretion, at least until I

know the situation on the ship. Twenty-four hours, maybe forty-eight, then we can reassess."

"We? You're suggesting me? No." She shook her head. "Definitely not. I can't." Her eyes grew big, panicked maybe, but she shielded them with a downward sweep of her lashes. "I really can't. It's impossible. No. Sorry."

Because of their history. Because he'd just been a bastard about it. *Damn it.* There was a reason he didn't make promises to women: he couldn't keep them, not the emotional kind. He didn't have it in him to fulfill and make happy. Not in a romantic way. In other ways…

He thought fast. "Look at what you gain. This is the son of the Makricosta chain of hotels and resorts. Do you recognize how much favor will be bestowed on the person who keeps him from harm? How do you feel about working cruise lines? Gideon has another ship launching next fall. You're climbing ladders so I assume your career is still very important to you. You'll be able to write your own ticket, Jaya. Anything you can't do, Adara will pay for you to learn. Hell, name your price and I'll pay it to know that I've got someone I can trust for the next few days."

"To babysit." Her mouth stayed in a flat, grim line of disgust.

"They're the toughest guests to please. Free dinner goes nowhere with them."

"Am I supposed to be laughing? Because I don't find this funny."

"Look, I know it sounds sexist. That's not why I'm asking. You're good with kids. Or does it bother you that I'd offer you money to help me?"

"Your being here bothers me, Theo," she snapped, turning her face away. "This is…" Her brow flinched into anguish.

Her anxiety was a kick in the chest, especially as he sensed that her refusal wasn't coming entirely from being scorned. There was a fear component. Something more emotional. It occurred to him there might be a man in her life making her hold back.

His insides shrunk to knotted pieces of rawhide. He couldn't bring himself to ask if that was the problem. He didn't want to know.

"It's a big favor, I realize that," he managed.

She choked out a laugh. "Is that what this is? A favor? A professional courtesy?"

"It's an appeal to your better nature. Think of the children."

"Are you serious right now?" She pursed her mouth in a furious white line.

"Jaya, I can't afford mistakes. Letting a stranger look after these kids would be wrong. I need *you*. Tell me what it will cost. I'll pay it."

CHAPTER FIVE

JAYA'S EMOTIONS ROSE and fell on his words along with her temper. *Think of the children.* Really. *Really?*

As for mistakes, he obviously thought they'd made one. The truth was the complete opposite.

Her eyes kept gravitating to Androu. The resemblance was startling. Her family was supposed to be the one with the cookie-cutter genetics that stamped out cousins who could ride each other's passports. To see so much of Theo in his nephew threw her for a loop and she was already in a tailspin at seeing the man himself.

One glimpse of the sky pilot with his broody expression behind mirrored aviators and she'd turned into a lovestruck schoolgirl again. Never mind that she'd spent the past year and a half taking on responsibilities she'd never dreamed herself capable of shouldering. Men had been completely off her radar, given her being needed so much at home. She'd shut down thoughts of a future with Theo when he had neglected to return her few calls. She hadn't felt sexy and romantic anyway. She'd been tired and grief-stricken and determined to continue her career for the sake of her pride.

Finally, in the past few months, things had begun to settle into a routine. She'd felt good, if wistful, at the way things had turned out. She was empowered and in control: the independent, worldly, modern woman she'd always longed to be.

And yet she'd leaped to respond to Theo's text and had grown breathless watching his athletic frame tether his helicopter. Her eyes kept stealing glances at his leather bomber jacket and black jeans that were old enough to be scuffed gray in all the right places, accenting the muscles of his thighs. He was tough and aloof and as quietly commanding as always, framing his demands with that polite, *I need. I need a file, I need lunch at one, I need you, Jaya. I need you to care for my babies.*

Her heart lurched.

"I need to think," she mumbled, even though this situation was beyond comprehension. Her mind was going a mile a minute, trying to figure out what to do. Where was Saranya when she needed her cousin's sensible advice? *Why did life have to keep throwing such hard curves in front of her?*

No time for a pity party, she reminded herself as Oscar turned into the underground parking garage and stopped next to the elevators.

They'd arrived at Theo's *discreet* accommodation. She hadn't known what to think of that text, but she hadn't been able to ignore it. You didn't slam doors in this business no matter how badly you wanted to. He was right about her interest in her professional development. She had plans and one affair eighteen months ago wouldn't derail them—no matter how life-altering the consequences had turned out to be.

Besides, she had told herself when the text had popped up, *he was probably making the request on behalf of a favored guest.* When she'd climbed into the limo, she'd told herself not to expect Theo at the private airstrip. She'd braced herself for a mistress.

Talk about special guests who needed personal attention!

As they rode up the elevator, she sent him yet another glance of exasperation. They each carried a child. He had the bag of minimal groceries in his hand and was looking at her. His narrowed brown eyes sent a prickle of heat into her center.

No. They weren't starting that again. She'd learned her lesson, thanks. Looking away was like ripping off a bandage, but she mentally scoffed, *Think of the children.*

Although, when it came to advancing your career through favors for influential guests, he was right that they didn't come bigger than this. Managing this gorgeous hotel on the Mediterranean coast was fun and fulfilling, but if she pulled off keeping both the Marcussen Media and Makricosta Resort heirs off the paparazzi radar, she'd have it made in the shade. Paris, London, New York... She could name her price.

As they entered her hotel's best suite, she automatically searched for flaws that needed correction, but the eclectic mix of 1960s reproduction furniture, pop art, and ultramodern amenities awaited judgment with quiet perfection. Where many of France's oldest hotels were rabbit warrens of tiny rooms with even tinier beds, this one had been upgraded into chic suites of fewer rooms that catered to a very affluent clientele. An open space in the middle of the sitting room would be perfect for the babies to play. Since a curved breakfast bar was the only partition to divide the kitchenette from the adjoining dining area, they'd be in sight while their meals were made.

She couldn't have planned it better, she decided, glancing at the impossible-to-scale glass fencing around the pool deck. There were even child safety locks on the glass doors that led to the pool's edge.

If only she didn't have the sense she was approaching one of those crossroads she and Theo had talked about that night in Bali.

Don't think about it, she warned herself. He obviously didn't reminisce about what they'd shared. The memories twinkling through her like fairy dust needed to be blown off, swept up and dumped in the bin.

"This kid stinks," Theo said, pulling her back to the present and brutal reality.

"I'll order some diapers and show you how to change him," she said, refusing to be moved by the kicked puppy look he sent her.

He tried to put Androu down, but the tyke clung on, demanding to be held.

"Seriously kid, you stink."

"He's scared," Jaya provided. "Almost as scared as you."

His head went back and a mask of aloof dismissal fell over his features.

Oh, had that penetrated his thick shell? Rather than bask in satisfaction, she suffered a twinge of conscience. Deliberately insulting people wasn't her thing. She'd been on the end of too many bullying tactics herself.

And Theo's discomfort with having care of these two babies wasn't funny. It broke her heart. He really wasn't keen on children.

Still, she couldn't help noticing with a pang, "He trusts you. Do you spend a lot of time with him?"

"Whenever I'm in New York," he shrugged. "Adara's always inviting me to dinner and handing him off to me. I copy what Gideon does and we get along okay. Airplane rides, right, sport?"

Androu grinned, put out his arms and tipped forward into space, trusting he'd be caught with a firm hand under his chest. He made a raspberry noise with his mouth as Theo did a slow circle and dive with him.

Jaya took it like a punch in the stomach. Turning away from the heart-wrenching sight of Theo playing with the boy, she carried Evie to the sofa and started an animated movie on the television for her.

"Think you can handle them while I make a few calls?"

"You'll stay then," he said as though it was a done deal, but she read the underlying tension in his intense stare.

She wavered, still annoyed that he was only here because he wanted a favor, not because he wanted to see her, but a little voice inside her said, *Quit pretending you have a choice.* All the safe, secure blocks and fences and supports she'd put under and around herself trembled in warning of a bigger shake-up, but it had been destined to happen sometime. Today was as good an opportunity as any.

It was so hard to be near him, though. He still got to her, so handsome despite being stubbled and rumpled and smelling faintly of leather and fuel and sweat. Maybe because he looked so nonplussed and human. Like he genuinely needed her. Again.

He wasn't interested in her, she reminded herself, hurt even though she shouldn't be. He'd warned her not to expect more than their one night. She hadn't. It wasn't like she'd been in love with him. Not deeply, anyway. Just tentatively.

No, it was the fact he hadn't called when she'd had a serious reason to reach out to him. He shouldn't have dismissed her like some ditzy woman who didn't understand the rules. When he had texted her today with his cryptic message, she had responded. She expected that same consideration from him. He should have called her back.

He should know that he had his own baby who liked airplane rides.

Theo spoke to Gideon while Jaya chattered in French, ordering supplies to be delivered to their suite. When she began speaking Punjabi, she lost him, which irritated him further than he already was.

Forcing himself to pay attention to his own call, he heard

Gideon say, "It's a stunt. The son of an African prince. He's chasing down his runaway wife, although the guns are real and so are the consequences. We're stationary while the French and Spanish navies draw straws on whose jurisdiction we're in. Of course the FBI wants a say because we have so many Americans on board. Meanwhile, our pirate is threatening to draw all of North Africa into the fight if we don't turn over his wife, but if she's stowing away, we haven't found her. The ladies are having kittens that I sent the babies off the ship. Are they all right?"

"Safe," Theo replied, eyeing Jaya as she toed off her shoes and shrunk by a couple of inches. Something in her expression seemed disturbingly vulnerable as she spoke with a lilt of persuasion into her phone. Her tone riled up oddly protective instincts in him when, on the surface, she looked more self-assured than ever.

Again he wondered if there was a man in her life, then cut off his speculation. The thought of her with a lover made him nauseous.

"Can you keep them out of sight?" Gideon continued. "Nic's planning a broadcast from his cabin—man can't stand to be scooped—but we want to leave the impression they're still here, otherwise…"

"Understood. We're off the grid."

"Excellent. We're a day from shore once we can move again and may have to wait for a slip in Marseilles. I'll be in touch with an arrival time."

Theo ended the call, mind eased that his siblings and spouses weren't in immediate danger. Now he just had to—

A knock sounded and Jaya lowered her phone to motion at Theo. "That will be the bellman with the things I asked him to bring up. Take Androu to the bedroom while he brings everything in."

Evie was rapt with her princess movie, dark head below the sofa back. He stepped out of the main room and continued to watch her as he listened to Jaya direct a pair of young men to leave everything inside the door. She continued her call as they left.

After hanging up a moment later, she walked him through his first diaper change, then briskly began moving objects to higher ground and double checking that doors were locked, particularly the one to the pool deck.

"We could swim with them later. They'd like that," she murmured, sounding distracted, her nervous tension palpable. Maybe because he was hovering, but he couldn't help himself. He told himself it was the new experience of child-minding. Androu still clung with determined little fists and tight legs which was a disturbing feeling that reinforced to him how inadequate he was with the task of reassurance. All Theo could do was hold him and follow Jaya around.

He wasn't used to her taking an avoidance tack, though. In Bali, she had looked him in the eye and smiled every time he caught her eye, then blushed and shied maybe, but she'd never refused to meet his gaze. Her brisk movements around the flat were as much about putting distance between them as securing the space for the children.

Aware he was seeking his own sort of reassurance, he made himself halt in one spot and quit tagging after her like a lost puppy, but he couldn't stop himself from watching her slender limbs and smooth efficiency. He couldn't help remembering that her skin had smelled like cloves and almonds and her hair had been a cool weight of silk that had warmed against his bare chest.

She paused to scan the equipment littering the entrance.

"That seems like a lot of stuff. Two highchairs and a booster?" It looked like there were three portable cots, not that he was an expert on baby furniture.

"We can deal with this later. What did your brother-in-law say?"

He brought her up to speed and she nodded jerkily. "So

a couple of days. You're really sure you want me here? I'll have to spend the night. That means—"

"It's an imposition, I realize. Do you—" He swore under his breath, unable to put off asking. He didn't even want to know, but it might help control his still thriving attraction. "Is there someone in your life this will affect?" he forced himself to ask.

She stilled, not looking at him. After a long second, she nodded. Then she lifted an expression that was frozen between tortured and fretful.

He swallowed, surprised how deeply the knife thrust and twisted even though he'd braced for it. Even though she had every right to get on with her life. He certainly had no right to possessiveness. This situation was going to be unbearable.

Let her call an agency.

Before he could work up the will to make the concession, soft, pitiful whimpers rose over a lullaby being sung on screen. Evie's sobs turned into a heart-wrenching wail that made Jaya's eyes pop. She rushed toward the girl.

"Baby, what happened? Did you hurt yourself?"

Theo lowered his lids in a wince. "I didn't realize what you'd put on. That's Rowan's voice as the fairy godmother."

Jaya gathered up the toddler in a cuddle and murmured words of comfort. Her swift loving care to a child she barely knew struck into his toughened heart like an axe, leaving a wound that gaped and ached. He'd just realized how perfect Jaya was on the heels of learning she belonged to another man. She *should* be with someone. She deserved to be happy.

He still hated himself for never calling her back. He'd never felt so alone and lonely—and he knew loneliness like other people knew the lyrics to a favorite song.

With his breath burning his lungs, he asked, "What should we do?"

He meant, *Should we call in someone else?* But she only rocked Evie and said, "There's nothing we can do. Little ones need their mamas." Her brow flinched before she tried to distract Evie with a cheerful, "But we could go swimming. Do you like to swim?"

The bait and switch worked and after waiting for swimsuits and special diapers, they all climbed into the pool. Again Jaya was a natural, showing him how to hold Androu and coach him to kick while Evie proved to be part mermaid, pushing herself free of Jaya's grip and swimming to the edge where she came up to grin proudly.

It was a surprisingly conflict-free hour as he shifted his focus onto the moment and the safety of the children. Okay, he was also pretty damned aware of Jaya's nipples poking against the wet cups of her modest one-piece black swimsuit, but thankfully the cool water kept his libido from responding too wildly. She was *way* off-limits, even further than when she'd worked for him, so he suppressed his interest as best he could.

They were back to their Bali roles, polite and capable of basic camaraderie as they discussed neutral topics like the children, the weather, and Marseilles.

Until she said, "Theo," with surprising gravity behind him.

"Yes?" he prompted, keeping his back to her as he boosted Evie toward the edge.

Ah, hell, he had his back to her. Inner tension came on so fast he felt like he solidified and fractured in the same breath.

The scars should have become less of an issue for him in the last year. His whole family had started coming to terms with their childhood, but he'd spent so many years clenching his teeth against it all that he couldn't bring himself to open up to any of his siblings about what was plain as the stripes on his back. There didn't seem any point and they were still so awkward with each other. He wanted to be friends with his older brother, but making that happen was easier if they both pretended the ugliness in their early lives hadn't happened. Maybe it was counterproductive, but all of them had been raised to be polite and ignore. They very easily fell back on that coping strategy.

Jaya was private and quiet, but she was soft. Anything that moved her started at heart level. If she asked him about this, it would be because she was concerned.

Knowing that made the cracks in him extend to even deeper places, touching into areas that were raw and sensitive. Thank God he had a baby to keep an eye on and didn't have to turn and face her pointed silence. He waited with ears that felt stretched and hollow, not ready for this conversation, not imagining he could ever be ready, but he didn't know how to avoid it.

After a long interminable moment, she asked, "What happened to your back?"

Ensuring Evie was out of the water and sitting safely on the edge, he kept a hand on her tiny frame and glanced at Jaya, dreading her pity.

Her anxious frown was so kind it made him want to shudder, like he'd had too big a taste of sugar. He swallowed back a thickness in his throat and was left with the bitter residue of a bleak time when he'd been insignificant and helpless.

"Exactly what you imagine happened," he answered in as controlled a tone as he could manage. Maybe he should have seen a counselor by now, but why? The emotional scars were as permanent as the physical ones. All he could do was accept them and try not to feel ashamed. He was smart enough to know it wasn't his fault, even if he'd grown up believing he must have done something to deserve all that abuse.

"Who—? When…? *Why?*" she choked.

"My father." A shadow of chagrin touched him. Shame that he had been so reviled by his own flesh and blood. Surely that meant there was something wrong with him.

Swallowing, he tried to find his equilibrium. He stepped back and nodded at Evie, inviting her to jump and swim toward him. Once he'd caught her up safe against his chest, he forced himself to look into Jaya's appalled face again.

"He was drunk." He tried to say it matter-of-factly, but a taut line inside him vibrated, making him unsteady. "I didn't keep my brother in his room as I'd been told."

"That's…" She shook her head and he could imagine someone as tenderhearted toward children as she was couldn't comprehend such cruelty. "How old were you?"

He reached for his well-practiced technique of shutting down, wanting to shrug off the details, but he couldn't seem to make it happen. No one had ever invited him to talk about this.

His body shivered as though the water he stood in was full of ice. "Eight. That's why I don't drink. That's why…"

He didn't want to apologize for Bali. They'd been using each other, she'd said so, but she had wound up expecting more after all. He'd let her down. He hated failure, but he didn't have anything else to offer. Maybe if she understood that, she wouldn't hate him so much.

Squinting into the sunlight reflected off the water, he spoke in a graveled voice. "That night in Bali…Adara had called me earlier that day to tell me she'd contacted Nic. We hadn't seen him in years, not since we were kids. Before he left home, our lives were pretty normal and decent. After Nic was gone, both our parents drank. Our father became violent. I blamed Nic because I never paused to think about how we were all kids when it happened. He hadn't had a choice, either. I hadn't considered that he might have suffered in his own way. When Adara told me he had…"

He shook his head, remembering how everything had

skewed in his mind, falling in a jumble he couldn't make sense of. Then Jaya had arrived, sweet Jaya, soothing and earnest and warm, wanting to say goodbye. He hadn't been able to bear the idea of her leaving. All he'd wanted was to keep her close.

"It was a lot to process," he said, hoping his strong dose of self-deprecation hid the impact her sharing herself had had on him.

"I understand."

"Do you?" he asked gruffly.

He wasn't a talkative man. He didn't have drinking buddies or squash partners. Men didn't typically share their personal garbage anyway. Not with each other, but he'd entrusted Jaya with his emotional safety that night. Maybe he hadn't shared his inner dialogue, but when she'd lain against him, naked and soft, her breath caressing his neck and her hair tickling his arm, he'd wanted to.

He wanted that emotional safety net again. Craved it like air.

Bending her dark head over Androu, she said, "I'm lying. I don't understand how anyone can be cruel to someone smaller than they are. It upsets me."

She looked up and the unprecedented connection he'd felt with her in Bali manifested like a beam between them, pulling them toward each other. The urge to move close and cover her mouth with his own was almost irresistible. He could practically taste her papaya flavor, could almost feel the cool mango smoothness of her lips against his.

A buzzer broke the spell.

Jaya's expression fell to one that was appalled and startled before she buckled her shoulders in a cringe. She wasn't given to swearing as far as he knew, but she muttered something in Punjabi that might have been a curse.

"Who is it?" he asked, worried they'd suffered a leak to the press.

"Quentin. I asked him to bring…" Her look of remorse-ful appeal made all the sharp edges in him abrade against each other.

"Your things?" he guessed. "Understandable."

A ripping sensation went through him nonetheless, tear-ing away the paper walls he used to disguise the fact his childhood still affected him. He thought, *Lucky, lucky man,* and hated his rival for being smart enough to win her heart and keep it. The bastard had better be good to her.

He waved her to climb the stairs before him then had to avert his gaze from her ass and the backs of her long slen-der thighs. "Is he staying?" *There'll be a murder-suicide in tomorrow's papers.*

"I thought we'd have more time to talk before he ar-rived," she said, handing him a towel before wrapping An-drou like a Mexican burrito.

"What else is there to say?"

Her flashing glance was loaded as a hot pistol, but she only carried Androu inside. He followed on heavy feet, re-luctant to meet her…what was the beau's label? She wasn't wearing a ring so they weren't married or engaged. Maybe they were only dating.

"We'll swim more later," he promised Evie as she pro-tested leaving the pool to come inside. He paused to reach up and lock the door behind him as he entered, then forced himself into the foyer where more bags had landed among the flotsam there.

A stocky blond man chopped his German tirade short as he spied Theo over Jaya's shoulder. His blue eyes were sharp, his manner too damned proprietary.

Every male instinct came alive in Theo, despite having no claim on Jaya. He looked right into the man's eyes with challenge, mentally aware it was wrong, but he couldn't help himself. If the guy wanted her, he could damn well fight for her.

"So. You finally turn up," the German gruffed.

"Quentin, please." Jaya murmured as she turned to look at Theo. Her imploring eyes filled with compunction while she kept a hand in the middle of her paramour's chest. No, not on his chest. As she shifted, Theo saw the baby trustingly clutched in the man's curved arm.

Don't drop Evie, Theo reminded himself, but the sight of that mite with black hair, dusky skin and curious brown eyes was a kick in the gut. He was Jaya's. There was no mistaking the maternal protectiveness in her hand on the baby boy's tiny blue T-shirt.

Time stood still as he processed all of them standing there with babies in their arms, Quentin with his rumpled suit and grim expression, he and Jaya practically naked with towels around their waists. Yes, this was good and humiliating to meet the father of her child with his pants proverbially around his ankles and his ineptness with children on full display.

"Quentin is my cousin's husband. I told you about Saranya when I was leaving Bali. Do you remember?" Jaya asked.

"Of course." Not the father then. His mind cycloned as he attempted to process this new information. If Quentin wasn't the father, who was? To hide his inner chaos, he fell back on the scrupulous manners drilled into him as a child. "How is she?"

"Dead," Quentin said flatly.

Nice. Theo surprised himself by thinking he might understand Quentin's bitterness a little, given how agonized he was at the mere thought of Jaya not being available to him. He couldn't imagine how he'd react if she were beyond his reach in a grave.

"I'm sorry," he offered, aware how useless the words were, but it's what you said.

"You should be," the German growled.

I didn't kill her, Theo bit back, able to curb the desire to be cruel because Quentin wasn't involved with Jaya, but if he wasn't the man in her life, who was?

His gaze returned to the bright brown eyes that were almost familiar, yet not like Jaya's nearly black irises. A hit of déjà vu accosted him because he could have sworn he'd looked into those eyes earlier today...

The air dried up around him. His heart began to pound with thick hammer blows inside his chest. The kicked feeling in his gut tightened around a serrated blade that turned low and without mercy. If he had bones, they'd vaporized.

Don't. Drop. Evie. He rather desperately tried to recollect if Demitri had been to Bali or had business in Marseille last year.

"Will you please let me handle this?" Jaya's voice seemed to come from far away. She tried to take the baby from Quentin, but she already held Androu.

For the life of him, Theo couldn't approach and take his nephew, even though he knew he should.

"Let you play house?" the German grumbled. "For how long? There's a reason you and Saranya were always railroaded by the men in your family. You *let* them."

"So if I tell you to butt out and leave, you will?"

Quentin gave her a stern look, but followed it with a resigned sigh that ended in a kiss on her cheek. He transferred the baby into her arms and straightened to throw another bitter glare at Theo.

The animosity in that look told Theo who the father was. Not Demitri. Hell, he didn't know if he should be relieved or not. How he stayed on his feet, he'd never know.

"Call me if you need me," Quentin said to Jaya and walked out.

Jaya took a shaken breath as the door closed, then turned to face him. The two boys she held weren't far apart in age and despite the slightly darker skin tone on the smaller one, and the black hair where Androu's was brown, their eyes and mouth were mirror images.

The sensation of dissolving from the inside out continued to assault Theo. He couldn't form a proper thought. He tried, but this was more than he could grasp. More than he wanted to believe.

"This is Zephyr," Jaya said, voice strained, but firm and a trifle defiant. "My...*our*...son."

CHAPTER SIX

THEO STARED AT her like she was a stranger. His wide tanned chest didn't seem to rise and fall at all where he clutched Evie in a towel against it. His lips were white and severe, his stillness frightening.

Accusation sharpened his level glare.

"I tried to tell you," she began, then thought, *No.* No remorse. He hadn't returned her calls. That's why this was a shock to him. If she hadn't found the right time to bring it up in the past hour, well, he'd had plenty of opportunities in the past year.

Nevertheless, a vision of the striped scars on his back flashed into her mind's eye. Her indignation deflated and their situation became a tangle again. How had they even got here, staring like a pair of cowboys waiting for the other to draw?

Her arms ached worse than her head, but not as bad as her heart.

"They're heavy," she said. "Can we move into the lounge?"

"Of course." He stepped forward and lifted Androu from her, averting his gaze from Zephyr's shy smile.

Zephyr was an engaging little chap, happy as anything, and Theo's turning away from him struck at the very core of her, setting her blood to boil.

Hugging her baby's tiny frame into her wet swimsuit,

she told herself to turn around and walk out, leave Theo to his "real" family.

Zephyr's connection to the other children stopped her. Without her own cousin's love and support, her life would be very different right now. Those sorts of ties were sacred to her and Zephyr wasn't likely to enjoy many of them with her side of the family. Her parents and siblings were even less inclined to speak to her now that she had a bastard soiling the family name.

Was Theo really as narrow-minded as they were, capable of rejecting a boy who hadn't done anything except have the gall to come to life inside her?

"Did you seriously just wet through this towel onto my arm?" Theo asked Androu in an aggrieved tone. "This kid hates me."

"He's a baby. They don't know how to be malicious." *So don't blame Zephyr if you're angry at me,* she added in a silent bite.

A tense twenty minutes passed as she took Evie and Zephyr into her bedroom to dress the girl and herself, leaving Theo charged with Androu. When she emerged, Theo wore a more truculent expression than any toddler. He held a naked Androu and a disposable diaper that looked worse for wear.

"This is why I'm not cut out to be a father," he charged. "I can't even manage the basics."

"Well, you are a father, so I guess you'll have to learn, won't you?" she shot back, heart wobbling in her chest at her own audacity. But this was one thing she wouldn't let the implacable Theo Makricosta block out. It was too important, and not just to Zephyr.

"I wasn't supposed to be. You *promised.* You said it would be a disaster—"

"Zephyr is not a disaster. Do *not*—" She cut herself off from raising her voice, looking away for a second to gather herself, afraid she'd frighten the children if she gave in to the press of emotions strangling her. Tears were right behind the anger so she swallowed hard, trying to keep it all from releasing.

"We're all frazzled and hungry," she managed in a croaking voice. "I called room service while we were changing. I'll dress Androu and once we feed the little ones and they're settled, I'll explain. All right?"

He glared, but didn't argue. An hour later, as she scrubbed faces and hands, he washed his own hands and grumbled, "I'm wearing more than they ate."

"It's better than wearing *what* they ate," she countered, not sure how they'd managed to be such a well-coordinated team when they were barely speaking. He'd let her lead, which surprised her, copying her actions with great care and concentration, as if there was a perfect system for feeding a baby.

It was such a contradictory vision of him and did funny things to her heart. He was so gloriously inept, but so determined to master these little child-care tasks. Like he'd suffer terribly if he failed to do it right.

Get smacked, maybe. With a belt.

Oh, Theo. Her throat filled with words she couldn't voice.

"That's gross," he replied after taking a moment to get her meaning about what the kids ate.

"It's reality," she murmured, lifting Zephyr from his chair and adding, "Do you want to watch them in the other room or finish cleaning up in here?"

As the older pair toddled off in two directions, he gave her a boggled look. "Maybe we should call an agency."

She tensed. So much for their tentative accord. "You don't want me and Zephyr here after all then." It was all she could do to pretend his rejection of their son didn't shatter her.

"No, I mean we need more help. This is a lot of work! Has either of us sat down since we walked in here four hours ago?" He skimmed a hand over his dry but uncombed hair and stabbed a look at Zephyr. "But now we've got this development to manage, too. Discretion is more important than ever, so I guess that leaves us stuck doing it ourselves."

"Development?" she repeated, hysterical laughter competing with outrage. *Stuck?*

"Who else besides your cousin's husband knows I'm— That you and I—"

"Made a baby?" she provided tartly. She tried to remember that he wasn't the most verbal person alive and this was all quite a shock for him, but honestly, why was it so hard for him to acknowledge his son? "Are you ashamed of Zephyr?" she guessed in a tone that thinned to outrage as the possibility sank in. It was the worst thing he could throw at her, striking directly into her Achilles heel. Into her soul.

"I'm shocked! You had to know I would be." He'd changed into a basic white T-shirt that strained across his chest as he gestured toward the view of the sea. "I can't have my family finding out through some cheap sensationalism on the internet. We've suffered enough secrets and lies as it is." He pinched the bridge of his nose.

Unwillingly, she felt sorry for him, which was crazy. He didn't deserve it, but, "I did try to call you when I first realized I was pregnant," she reminded.

He sighed, brows coming together in a pensive frown. "I debated calling you back, I did, but Adara turned up pregnant and given her previous miscarriages Demitri and I had to take over her workload. Then our mother died. By the time the dust settled, there didn't seem any point in contacting you."

They'd both been going through a lot. She supposed she couldn't fault him too much for not returning her calls under those circumstances.

"But I trusted you to take that pill, Jaya. What happened?"

The blame in his tone stabbed her, even though she'd tried to prepare herself for it every time she'd mentally walked through this conversation. Yes, she'd failed to protect both of them from the consequences of their night together and she was willing to own that, but his anger and disappointment filled her with umbrage. She didn't want to feel defensive and solely responsible. He knew what could happen from unprotected sex. It didn't matter that she had a better understanding of what had driven him that night. He had still chosen to sleep with her to satisfy his own selfish needs.

Just as, when it came down to it, she'd kept their baby for her own selfish reasons.

"The pill was expired," she explained with as much dignity as she could scrape together. "I thought I'd be able to get a fresh one once I landed in France, but with the time change and Saranya being so ill, it was days before I came up for air. By then I'd missed the window. Then I thought I'd wait to see if I had anything to worry about."

She flinched from the intensity of his judgmental stare, sinking bleakly back into that time of despair, feeling again the torn sensation of having said goodbye to her life in Bali, and Theo, then facing an even more brutal goodbye with her cousin.

Lifting her chin, she finished without apology, "When it turned out I was pregnant, I couldn't take steps to end it. I just couldn't, not with Saranya dying in front of me. I needed something to look forward to. The promise of life and love."

Scanning the lounge to ensure the older kids were staying out of trouble, she tried to hide that she'd also needed her connection to Theo to continue. Her conscience had tortured her over not keeping her word, but she wasn't sorry. Not one bit.

"I tried to tell you because you deserved to know." She cleared her throat. "I didn't, and don't, expect anything from you. Not money. Not marriage. He was my decision. He's my responsibility."

There. That's all she'd ever wanted to say, even though she had ached every day to share her pregnancy and baby with Theo. Zephyr was such a little miracle. She wanted Theo to love him as much as she did.

"Oh, sweetie, don't eat that—" she blurted, realizing Androu had picked lint out of the carpet.

Rushing forward was a much-needed break from the weight of Theo's gaze. She couldn't face him after what she'd just said and didn't want to see his relief at being absolved of any duty or involvement with his son.

Theo tried to find comfort in her letting him off the hook. God knew he didn't want to explore the miasma of primordial goo that bubbled inside him as he considered what it meant to be a father.

Inexplicably he was hurt, however. Stinging with rejection at her wanting nothing to do with him.

Fortunately, he was too busy to dwell on whether he should feel sorry for himself or not. Once the kitchenette was tidied, there were beds to set up and pajamas to be ordered, then everyone had to be threaded into them—which was like pushing a rope up a staircase.

"I'm thinking we need bedtime stories and some stuffies. Do they have special blankets or sleeping toys? This could be a rough night," Jaya warned as she placed a call to a nearby shop before it closed.

"Unlike the day it's been?" he drawled, waving agreement to whatever she wanted to charge to the room.

He wasn't trying to fuel a fight. It struck him how painfully familiar this tension was, like a typical Makricosta gathering. They had a full-grown elephant between them in the shape of a dark-haired baby boy, but they remained civil, only speaking about the logistics of what needed to be done as they ran their mini-hotel. It should have been a relief, but he found the circumventing and pretending frustrating.

Was this his punishment for the mistake of not wearing a condom? Because he was feeling castigated, chastised and rebuked. Slapped around, knocked down and kicked to the curb.

Why? he found himself wanting to demand. *Why don't you want anything from me? Because you're afraid I'll screw up?*

He'd never been able to challenge his father, not without suffering worse for it, and he wasn't sure how to act around Jaya when he felt this abused. His primary instinct when his emotions were churned up was to isolate himself, but no luck on that score. It was all hands on deck and he was about as frayed and tired as the toddlers, barely keeping it together as he counted down the minutes to their bedtime.

If only Jaya would offer the same quiet reassurance she kept giving to the homesick tykes. He watched her adeptly keep them from shedding more than a few sniffles, relieved to know he'd made the right choice in tracking her down, but he was damned jealous of each cuddle and kiss she offered.

His gaze fell on Zephyr and he experienced the crack between the eyes that was his own egocentric vulnerability eighteen months ago. If only he could go back to the ignorance that had been bliss yesterday.

Not all the way back to Bali, though. He didn't regret making love to her.

Disturbed, he shifted his gaze to Jaya, worried she could read his betraying thoughts.

He wanted to resent her for letting him down, but after what she'd told him about her cousin, he couldn't find it in him to hate her for failing to take the pill. Maybe the promise of love and life hadn't been uppermost in his mind when his mother had been dying, but he had an inkling how helpless and hopeless she must have felt.

He couldn't judge her for using procreation as a coping strategy, either, could he? Not when he'd employed it with her—in a rather shortsighted manner—when he'd been under the duress of Adara's confession about Nic.

And where was the point in being angry about what she should have done? It couldn't be undone. The child was here.

Still, he couldn't face this, couldn't face fatherhood. What kind of an example had been set for him? Look at his back.

Not that the children had any idea how useless he was. Once they'd scattered their new toys across the blanket Jaya had spread on the floor of the lounge, Evie brought him a book.

"Jaya's the reader. I'm the sentry," he said, motioning to his sprawled body acting as a fence between the corner of a chair and the length of the sofa to keep them corralled.

"Peas," she implored with a heart-stealing smile, reeling him in an inch. Until today he hadn't spent much time with her, but she was the most gentle, tender thing he'd ever seen, enchanted with Baby Zepper, chattering like old friends to Androu, missing her parents and thus taking to Jaya with impulsive hugs and embraces.

"Sure, I'll read," Jaya said breezily. "If Uncle takes the next dirty bottom."

"Never mind. I got this." Theo sat up so his back was against the edge of the sofa.

Evie wormed herself into his side, making him lift his

elbow in surprise. The weight of her head felt surprisingly endearing as she let it droop against his rib cage.

He imagined she was just getting sleepy, but it still felt like a very trusting gesture, one that gave him a funny sensation of fullness around his heart.

As he started to read, Androu toddled over with a car clutched in his fist, drool glossing his chin. As he plopped down on Theo's other side, a drip fell to slide down Theo's wrist.

"Seriously, dude, I'm going to talk to your parents about your manners."

"He can't help teething," Jaya scolded, coming across with a tissue to dry the boy's face.

As she bent, Theo raised his hand so she could wipe the spit off his arm. Zephyr, balanced on her hip, read some kind of invitation from their body language and tilted out of her grip, reaching out with his short arms for Theo.

Jaya gasped, so caught by surprise she almost dropped the boy.

Theo had no choice but to catch him one-handed, guiding the boy into a safe landing against his chest. The tot flipped and slid into his lap like an otter down a log.

Distant base instincts cautioned him about the tiny feet kicking near his jewels, but a stronger, less easy to define reaction took over. He was shaken by the natural way Zephyr relaxed into him. It was passive aggression at its best, clashing into his protective inner walls with unseen yet gong-like reverberations. He'd been avoiding touching the boy, thinking he'd decide later whether he'd take an active part in the boy's life, after he'd figured out what to make of the situation and how many options he had.

He didn't want this puppy warmth sitting in his center, thawing the tight frozen pillars he used to brace himself against the world.

But when he looked up at Jaya, thinking to ask her to

take him, her expression was so vulnerable, so fearful of rejection on the boy's behalf, he couldn't do that to her. Hell, he couldn't do it to a child. To his *son.*

This situation was the most perplexing, dumbfounding circumstance of his life, but these little creatures were incredibly defenseless. Like her, he couldn't understand how anyone could hurt a child. He certainly couldn't do it himself.

Which didn't make him father material, he reminded himself, ignoring the clenched sensation around his heart. Kids needed a lot more than the basics of food and shelter and a soft place to sit. Nascent things like love were beyond him so she was setting him up for failure with Zephyr. That was not something he could easily forgive, but he couldn't hurt the boy out of anger with her.

Aware of Jaya standing over him, arms hugged across her middle, he refused to look up to see how she reacted to his playing human recliner.

"There was a farm up the road from my mother's house in Chatham," he said, trying for dismissive when he could hear the rattled edge in his tone. "I saw a sow there once, knocked over by her own piglets because they wanted to nurse. Now I know how she felt." He wasn't doing this because he wanted to, he implied. He had no choice.

He began to read aloud, silently willing her to go away. It was one thing to have his emotions hanging by a thread while children listened to him struggle through a story. They wouldn't know the difference, but Jaya was perceptive. He hated knowing she could tell how confused and defenseless this made him.

After a few seconds, she drew a hitched breath.

"Do you know if Androu has a bottle before bed? I'm going to make one for Zeph." Her voice was blessedly lacking in inflection.

"Text Adara and ask."

"Okay, but—" She started across to her phone. "What have you told her? Does she know I'm here?"

"I told Gideon I'd recruited you, but that was when we first got here. They don't know about..." He looked down at the dark head turning against his breastbone, more interested in the older babies and chewing his fist than the picture book.

Jaya didn't answer. He thought she was texting until he heard the familiar shutter-click of the camera app. He glanced up in dismay.

She shrugged. "This might never happen again." Her trim figure, encased in three-quarter length jeans and a lime-green shirt, disappeared toward the kitchenette.

He drew in a breath that burned his lungs, suddenly wondering whether he had any choice when it came to involvement in his son's life. Jaya might have made up her mind that *this might never happen again.*

CHAPTER SEVEN

"I CAN HONESTLY say this has been the most grueling day of my life," Theo said, flopping onto the sofa when he and Jaya came back to the lounge after settling all the babies.

"Try nineteen hours of labor," she chirped, picking up toys rather than sitting.

Guilt assailed him. He'd put his sister's pregnancy ahead of Jaya's. Unknowingly, sure, but at the time he'd convinced himself he was putting both women's best interests ahead of his own. Somehow he didn't think saying so would be an easy sell to the woman who'd struggled through childbirth alone.

"Was it bad?" he asked, bracing inwardly while leaning to gather the toys within reach.

"It wasn't a picnic, but it was fairly typical. He was worth it."

"That's what my sister says. I don't know how women do it." He searched her expression, awed that she wasn't berating him.

"You just do. There's no time to figure out how." Clenching a stuffed panda between her tense brown hands, she said, "Kind of like the way I sprang him on you. There wasn't any opportunity to prepare you, but you still seem furious so let's have it. Don't keep giving me the robot mode of being terribly polite. If you want to yell, yell. Except, don't wake the babies, but—" She sighed sharply. "I know you feel lied to, but I swear I didn't do it for money or to take advantage of you."

His heart turned over in his chest. He wished he could dismiss her as conniving. It would be so much easier to keep his own emotions out of it if she had none, but one of her main attractions for him beyond the physical had always been her earnest sincerity.

"I believe that money was the last thing on your mind."

Her smile of relief made him wish they could leave it there, but she needed to fully comprehend the rest. Leaning his elbows on his knees, he rubbed his face, trying to erase any sign of the turmoil still blowing like a hurricane inside him.

"But whether you want money or not, it's the only thing you'll ever get from me."

Her lips slacked in surprise, then pursed. Her brows drew together and she shifted her gaze to the darkened windows. "I don't want any."

"No, you want me to be a father, I can tell. But Jaya, that stuff I told you earlier about my lousy childhood. That's why I never wanted to be one." He looked past her knees, jaw clenching, seeing nothing but a blur of his past. "It's not just fear that I'll turn out like the old man and raise my hand—"

"You wouldn't," she said.

He lifted his gaze to focus on her face, trying to read her meaning. Was it a challenging, *You wouldn't dare?* Or an expression of confidence in him?

He mentally stepped away from trying to decipher her words, disturbed by how badly he wanted her to believe in him when he didn't know if he could believe in himself.

"I'd like to think I wouldn't, but if my life fell apart the way my dad's did and I tried to cope by drinking…" He rubbed the hard tension from his jaw, needing her to understand that whether she wanted something from him or not, there was nothing here. "Beyond that, though, is the lack of substance in me. I told you what kind of man I was that night in Bali. I'd make a terrible father. I don't make strong connections, ever. Kids need something better than what I'm capable of offering."

It was the hard truth, but he still searched her expression, wanting her to argue.

"Aren't you underestimating yourself?" Hope wound through her question like a strand of gold, catching at him, filling him with bittersweet satisfaction at how predictable she was. He wished he could live up to her view of him, he really did.

He shook his head. "The closest connection I have is with my sister and we don't talk about personal things." Well, he didn't. Adara had opened up about her marriage when it had almost fallen apart, but he'd only had to listen and stand by her. No reciprocation required.

"What about your brother? You said you talked to Adara about Nic that night we—I mean in Bali."

Inexplicably, he found himself rising, finding himself verging on retreat because her question stood on his toes and leaned into his space, but he couldn't walk out. He owed her some kind of explanation.

He tried to pace off his discomfort. "Adara talked, I listened. Since then I've told you more about how that has impacted me than I've ever admitted to anyone else."

"Really?" She cocked her head in surprise.

"This is what I'm saying, Jaya. I don't connect on a meaningful level. To be honest, I wish I *could* take a page from Nic's book. He grew up isolated and neglected and he's made a really good life for himself. A nice family with Ro and Evie. So has Adara with Gideon. I look at the way they dote on their kids and I'm envious, but I don't even know what words describe those things they demonstrate so how could I become like they are?"

She pressed her drawn lips together and swallowed like she was fighting back deep feelings. Her unblinking eyes glittered before she dropped her lashes to hide them.

"Not every man falls in love at first sight with his child," she allowed in a voice that made his heart shrivel. "It's different for a woman, especially when she carries the baby for nine months. The attachment is there from the minute she holds the baby."

"What if the attachment never arrives?" His worst nightmare was producing that same feeling of being unwanted and unloved that he'd grown up with. "What would that do to Zephyr if he expects it and it isn't there? Don't bother trying to answer that because I know how it feels. I thought I had an attachment to my father and he wound up attacking me with his belt."

She flinched like he'd struck her and he wanted to kick himself.

"I shouldn't talk to you about it." He paced away across the room. This was why he didn't talk about his personal life. "It upsets you to hear it and it doesn't do a damned thing to resolve it for me, but that's what I'm trying to get across. He broke that part of me. I don't know how to be what a child would need. I only know what not to be."

"That's a start."

"A very pitiful one. Zephyr deserves better. Be the mother I know you are and admit that. You wouldn't settle for anything less than the best for him."

She didn't say anything, only pressed her knuckles to her mouth and kept her head bent. She might even have nodded.

That hurt. It hurt so bad he couldn't breathe, even though—maybe especially because—it was the honesty he'd demanded.

"So let's talk about money," he said.

Her gaze came up, dagger sharp with disbelief. "I was

dead serious when I said the last thing I'd ever do is use
him to extort anything from you."

"That doesn't mean you'll never struggle. He's the only
progeny I'll have." He certainly wouldn't take any woman's
word and play roulette with his sperm again. He should
look into a vasectomy, he supposed, filing that thought for
later because right now he couldn't imagine sleeping with
anyone but the woman in this room.

Weird how he could be having this incredibly uncom-
fortable conversation and still be aroused by the way her
breasts moved in the confines of her bra or her pants clung
to her backside as she bent.

Forcing himself to set down thoughts too hot to entertain, he said, "Whether you want it or not, I'll set up a port-
folio for both of you. You might as well have a say in it."

"Oh, Theo! I was going to leave Zephyr with Quentin
tonight." She sprang into action again, tossing soft bears
and cloth books into a box that groceries had been delivered in. "Then I saw how much poor Evie and Androu were
missing their mamas and I couldn't deprive Zephyr of a
night with his own. And I was mad at you! I was mad that
you ignored my calls because I never wanted your stupid
money or a relationship or anything for *me.* I only wanted
to be decent and let you know you have a son. And now
what are you doing? Offering me money and trying to pretend your child doesn't exist."

"I didn't say that," he growled, pushing angry fists into
his pockets, slouching as he turned his back on her. "That's
not what I said."

"Then take part in his life!"

"How? I've just explained that I don't want to hurt him,
physically or mentally, but I very likely would!"

"But that's it, that's the vital piece you think you don't
have. You already care about him. Don't you? A little?"
Don't beg, she warned herself. He might be right. It might

be better to buffer Zephyr against indifference if that's all Theo was capable of.

She really didn't want to believe that, though. She didn't want her son growing up feeling as she had, dismissed and unimportant. For heaven's sake, didn't he realize what a gift she'd given him? A *son.* That was supposed to elevate *her* value in his eyes.

Congratulations, Jaya. Modern women raise their children alone and *nobody* regards her as special. The clash of cultural mores made her furious.

"Don't write Zephyr off without even trying to get to know him. That's callous. It's cowardly. You be a better man than that," she demanded with a point of her finger. "I never would have slept with you if I believed you lacked compassion and the ability to respect someone for their worth."

"Really." He spun to confront her, head thrown back in challenge as he stared down his nose at her. "I thought we were using each other for escape that night."

And he was getting his back up because he thought she'd been after a deeper relationship after all. Maybe, yes, way down she had feelings for him that longed to be requited, but she shook her head vehemently.

"No. I mean yes, I was using you. But I wouldn't have used a man less decent than you are."

He barked out a disbelieving laugh. "Nice."

"That didn't come out right. I'm saying that I didn't expect to have sex with you, but it happened because I respect you. And I'm not sorry. I'm happy we made Zephyr. I was resigned to not having children so…" She was saying too much. With a pleat stressing her brow, she clammed her mouth and decided they'd talked enough for one night.

"Really?" He tucked in his chin. "You're the most natural person I've ever seen with kids. Was there something wrong that made you think you couldn't have any?"

They'd definitely talked enough.

"I told you my career was important to me," she mumbled, casting about for the last of the toys, but they'd tidied up all of them.

"And you still have a career despite being a single parent. Not always an ideal situation, I'm sure, but I can't believe you didn't see before Zephyr that kids and career can coexist. You must have considered it an option. You didn't say you weren't *planning* to have kids, but that you resigned yourself not to, like you didn't think it was possible. Are you okay, Jaya? Because my sister may not have confided all the trauma of her miscarriages, but I'm aware there can be complications with any pregnancy. It makes me a real bastard for not protecting you that night if I put your life at risk."

"Have you listened at all? I was textbook normal. I'm made to have babies and I'm not sorry I had him. Not one bit. That's all I meant. Now we should get some rest. Even if they sleep through the night—which they won't—they'll be up early." She tried to scoot past him.

He caught her arm.

She caught her breath.

Silly, silly Jaya. Still flushing like a preteen at this man's touch. Shyness kept her face averted. She didn't want him to see how much he still affected her.

His thumb brushed her bare skin, hot palm leaving an imprint of his firm but gentle grip. *Those hands.* Knowledge burned in a trail from the light caress of his thumb to the pit of her stomach and lower, flooding her inner thighs with tingling warmth. Her face stung with the pressure of a hard blush.

He cleared his throat and pulled his touch away like he felt the scald. When he spoke, he didn't pursue the other topic, but floored her with something else.

"When I asked if there was someone in your life, I meant

a man. Is Zephyr it, or is there someone else I should be worried about?"

"Would you be?" she asked, snapping her head up then regretting it. He must be able to read the flush of awareness savaging her, but he looked his old, contained self.

"This is complicated enough without navigating some other man's sense of claim." So aloof. So hands-off. She was back in Bali, heart tattooing her breastbone like a moth against a window, trying to reach the light.

She looked away and rubbed the feel of his touch from her arm. "No, there's not. What about you?" The question escaped as the horrifying thought occurred.

"Are you kidding? No."

"Still playing concierge for the Lonely Hearts Club?" she sniped, annoyed.

"Open to new members. Always."

Ouch. She set her jaw, trying not to let his flippancy bother her. He was only trying to prove his shallowness. Maybe he is that shallow, Jaya. *There's not a woman in the world with enough training to fix me. Don't try.*

She needed to believe he was better than what he was pretending though, she needed it like oxygen. It was how she had let down her guard with him that night. Yes, his rakish ability to give her pleasure had made the memories he'd given her particularly delicious, but her trust in him had been the groundwork. She had believed him to be a good, honorable man, which had allowed her to put herself in his care.

"Don't be less than you are, Theo."

"Don't imagine I'm more."

"I'm only expecting you to be you, the man who saw potential in me and gave me a chance to develop it. You're fair. You're kind. Sometimes you're funny. This isn't a test. You don't have to pass it right now. We have a few days. Apparently," she added with a jerky shrug. "Can't we use this time to figure out how to proceed? Do we have to spit out a settlement contract this evening so you can run out the door tomorrow? Maybe the reason you don't have close relationships is because you don't stick around to nurture them."

He rocked back on his heels. "Touché."

"Was that harsh?" she asked, not as repentant as she could have been.

"No, it's true. I'm as much of a moving target as I can make myself."

The reasons behind that coping strategy put a lump in her throat. She tried to swallow it back with little success.

"Well, this is a safe place," she reminded in a strained tone. "You made sure. No one can hurt you here."

For a few seconds she thought she might have gone too far, appealing to the frightened child in him.

His dry chuckle had a coarse edge. "Okay, sure. I suppose we're stuck here," he said without inflection. "No need to rush to act."

Stuck again. Reacting to that awful word, she said, "There are worse things than taking a day off to play with children, you know."

"I know." His shoulders slumped heavily.

Now she really did feel sorry, but he walked away before the apologetic hand she reached out could touch him.

It was a sleepless night and not just because he had to walk Androu twice. Theo's mind wouldn't stop so he was grateful to have a reason to pace. The boy's warm weight on his arm was oddly comforting as he patted his little back to soothe him.

Jaya had to show him how, of course, demonstrating on Zephyr. "He might be with me, but it's still a strange place," she whispered in explanation of the boy's restlessness. She settled him with expert swiftness and disappeared into her room.

He dragged his eyes off the way her hotel-issued robe draped the curve of her hips and showcased her slender calves. No man in her life and whose fault was that? His. He'd taken a chance with unprotected sex because he'd been anxious to lose himself and his problems in an orgasm.

Which wasn't entirely true. As he stared across the twinkling lights of Marseille to the dark expanse of the Med, he allowed that Jaya had never been like the other women he pursued. She was special. His need that night had been as much about a desire to be with her as it had been to escape his emotional turmoil. Her announcement she was leaving Bali had lit a torch of panic in him. He'd needed, quite literally, to hold onto her.

Maybe some primitive part of him had even been seeking the permanent connection of a blood tie. As much as he'd like to dismiss his failing to protect her as a state of crisis and thoughtlessness, he'd never neglected a condom in his life. He *always* thought ahead to consequences. Fear of a beating had predisposed him to it.

So he couldn't pretend he'd simply been carried away. He'd made a conscious decision to take a risk.

Creating a child without due care and attention seemed like the kind of enormous mistake he ought to be punished severely for. His body was reacting with the same tense anticipation of hell he'd grown up trying to ignore. The clogged chest, clogged throat and anxiety ought to be far behind him, but he could hardly breathe. Sleep had never been a safe escape. Voices could rise in the next room, furniture could topple. Babies could wake and nightmares became real.

The troubling memories kept him tossing and turning even after Androu settled. Then Evie woke like a five alarm fire, jarring him and making his heart pound.

No male voice shouted, though. No impossible demands were made of children barely old enough to reach a toaster.

Jaya worked her magic and scooped up the sad little girl, murmuring reassurances.

Androu wasn't happy about being woken from a sound sleep, but Jaya distracted him with a bottle then cuddled the pair into a nest of pillows and blankets on the floor in the lounge, a cartoon of sleepy baby animals flickering at low volume on the television.

"Maybe they'll fall back asleep. Listen for Zephyr while I have a quick shower?"

He was used to starting his day shortchanged on sleep because of a time zone shift, but he'd barely slept and it wasn't even six o'clock yet. No wonder new parents were so irritable.

A few minutes later, as he searched out the coffee in the kitchen, he heard a cry. It wasn't from either of the toddlers. As he moved into the hall, the unhappy sounds grew louder. Pushing into Jaya's room, he found Zephyr sitting up in his cot with big tears on his cheeks, eyes wide and lost.

It's not a test, Jaya had said, but it was. Not just of his fatherly instincts, of which he had none, but of his ability to keep his emotional blocks from damaging this baby.

Therefore, inadequate as he felt, he couldn't leave the tyke wet and scared to wait for his mother just because she knew how to reassure with affection and he didn't.

At least a diaper change was his first priority. Funny how that seemed like a reprieve from more demanding tasks. Surprisingly, he nailed it in one go. Even got the kid back into his jammies without misaligning any snaps.

Zephyr seemed to want to keep his blanket with him, so Theo wrapped it around the boy's tiny body and snugged him closer to the warmth of his own chest, concerned that the air conditioning was set too low in the lounge.

Whether it was the warmth of his body or he was still sleepy, he seemed content enough to be carried into the lounge.

The older babies had both dropped off and Theo found himself standing over them, Zephyr's silky hair under his chin smelling familiar even though it wasn't anything he really knew.

Babies were unwieldy responsibilities that were so great, they were to be run from, far and fast. That's what he'd believed and it was true, if you were five.

He was an adult, though, perfectly capable of things like changing a diaper and making a proper meal and laundering clothes. Fearing the responsibilities of fatherhood was irrational. Millions did it every day and no one would hold him accountable with a beating if he missed getting a bit of food out of a kid's hair during a bath.

Nevertheless, after his talk with Jaya last night, his terror at taking on the role of a father was worse, not better. He knew why, too. He still feared failing, but not because of the threat of violence. He couldn't stand the idea of disappointing Jaya.

Jaya came out of her bathroom to find Zephyr's cot empty and rushed out to the main room where she found Theo cradling their son like he'd been doing it all his life.

Her blood thickened to such sweet molasses, she couldn't move. Her limbs ached and felt weak.

She must have gasped because he glanced up and touched a finger to his lips, then tilted his head to see into Zephyr's tranquil face. In slow motion, like he was handling a chemical bomb, he tucked Zephyr next to his sleeping cousins on the floor and drew their blanket over him.

She was done. Finished. Melted into a puddle on the floor that housekeeping would have to mop up and wring out of the strings.

He added a final blow by fetching his phone off the dining table and snapping a picture of the children piled together like a litter of kittens.

Removing the hand she'd pressed to her mouth, she accused in a whisper, "You're sentimental."

He shrugged, striding toward the kitchenette where he set his phone on the table and began making coffee. "We're not likely to catch them all together like that again, are we? Not all asleep."

The breath she took was coated in powdered glass. "I thought about sending the photo from last night to your sister, but you haven't told her, have you? Will you?"

He slowed his movements. "Since she's my boss and it starts with explaining that I slept with an employee—"

"Not technically."

He kicked up a brow, unimpressed with the fine line. "Still not the best example." He pushed the button that started the espresso maker. "And I'm still wrapping my head around it. I'd rather keep things simple until I know how we're going to proceed."

She tried to hide her disappointment, then thought, *Why should I?*

"That's not really fair to Zephyr, is it? I mean, they're his cousins." She waved at the bumps under the blanket. "My relationship with Saranya was the most important of my life." Not an understatement. "We grew up together and when I needed her, she was there. You don't just call a cousin out of the blue when your life implodes. Not unless you've been close all along."

She braced against his asking her how her life had imploded, but he only folded his arms and hitched a hip against the counter.

"I didn't think of it like that. I keep thinking how much they're like us. The age mix is different, of course. I'm barely a year younger than Adara and Demitri is almost four years younger than me, but we were only a few years older than Evie and practically left to raise ourselves. Adara was all I had for a mother figure and she was looking after

Demitri. I guess some part of me thought it was too much to ask of Evie and Androu to take on Zephyr, but they have functioning parents."

"So does he," she reminded, wishing she could be amused by his almost naïve misreading of the situation, but it was so tragic. "Is that why Adara always seems so…" She searched for the right word to describe her former boss that wouldn't insult the whole family. "I always thought you and she seemed very introspective."

He snorted. "You mean aloof? Distant? Cold? I've been called worse and yeah, we're not the most demonstrative family, but Adara did the best she could. I can't fault her. I'd do anything for her."

Ignoring the pang of jealousy that struck, she listened deeper, hearing exactly how far he was willing to go on his sister's behalf.

"Did you step in to protect her from your father?" Part of her knew she shouldn't ask. She didn't want to open up her own wounds and show them off so she couldn't expect him to, but her heart ached for the boy he'd been.

He flinched and turned away to set a tiny cup on a silver saucer. "Not that it did much good. She still caught her share. Demitri was the one we worried about. He was so little."

"Oh, Theo. And you think you're not cut out to be a father?"

"Have you seen how Demitri turned out? If that's my work, I'd be scared. The man's a menace." He offered her the first coffee.

"You have that one. I like mine with steamed milk." She stepped into place before the machine and filled the receptacles. "And yes, I have met your brother. Thank goodness for the repellant that is the Makricosta uniform because we all would have been pregnant. He's very adept with the ladies."

"Were you attracted to him?" His sharp gaze made her very aware of her nakedness under the robe she'd pulled on when she'd realized Zephyr had been stolen from his cot.

"I can't deny he's good-looking, but no, not really attracted." *Not the same way I'm attracted to you.* She pretended that the spurt of coffee and steamed milk required close attention, using it to hide the betraying longing she shouldn't be feeling toward him.

"A year and a half ago you weren't dating because your career was too important. Now Zephyr's in the way, isn't he?"

"I wouldn't put it like that, but he's definitely a factor. I'm not about to introduce a string of men into his life. So yes, between him and what's been going on at home and starting my new job I haven't had time to date. But dating has never been a priority so I don't miss it." There, that glossed nicely over her reasons for still avoiding men.

Yet here she stood, vulnerable in a thin robe held closed by a slippery tie, in the presence of a virile man who could overwhelm her without even trying.

Would he try? She sidled her gaze over his broad chest. He was wearing yesterday's shirt that still had some of his nephew's supper on it. That made him seem very human and normal. If he crushed her against that stained cotton, her heart would sing.

When she glanced up, she found him staring into the part of her lapels where her upper chest was exposed. Behind the light satin of the robe, her nipples tightened. Why him, she wondered, but didn't actually care. It was just such a delightfully good sensation to react to a man.

With a harsh inhale, he visibly pulled himself together and looked away. "Are you still sending money home?"

Her sensual curiosity drained away.

"Yes." She didn't elaborate and deliberately put space between them, taking her coffee to the breakfast bar and positioning herself so she could see the kids if they moved. Partly it was decent child minding, but at a deeper level, she was confused and trying to figure out why she longed for Theo to make a move on her when she was still stinging from his dropping her from his life.

"Have you told *your* family about Zephyr?" he asked.

A spike of grief pierced her as fresh as the day her family had first shunned her, hanging up on her because she had dared to run away to live with Saranya, rather than stay in the ruin they all considered her life had become. "Put it this way. If you don't acknowledge him, my cousin's daughter and Quentin are his only support after me."

Silence. When she glanced back, he was scowling toward the lounge, arms folded in frustration. "There are plenty of people with old-fashioned views in America, but it still surprises me they'd ostracize you for having a baby out of wedlock."

She sipped her coffee, ignoring the opening to tell him it was more than that. She shouldn't feel ashamed, but there was also the bit where she'd have to explain that the steps she'd taken to leave India weren't entirely legal.

"Would—"

He didn't continue so she dragged her gaze to his again, finding him looking something like he had that night in Bali: slightly defensive, rumpled but gorgeous in spite of it. His jaw was stubbled, his hair disheveled, but his proud bearing and those hollow cheeks above a strong jawline made him one of those men who would get better looking with age.

There was no sign of uncertainty in his tall, solid stillness. His expression was impassive, as if he was asking after her plans for the day.

"Would it mend fences with your family if we married?"

He couldn't have hurt her more if he'd walked right by her yesterday at the hangar and pretended he didn't see her.

She wasn't a romantic. After being sexually assaulted, she had quit dreaming of the perfect man sweeping her off her feet with a proposal that made her cry happy tears—except possibly if it came from him.

Seriously, Jaya, you have to let this infatuation die.

But one thing she knew she wanted in any marriage proposal was for love to form the underpinning of it.

"Probably," she answered, forcing herself to reply honestly, but the word choked her. She had to sip at her coffee to clear her voice into working order. Eyes on the sleeping cherubs, she added, "But my country is full of women who married because they felt they had no other choice. I do have a choice and I'm not interested."

Another thick silence.

He had to be relieved, but she didn't glance over to interpret what he might be thinking. Her insides ached too much, especially near her heart. If he saw it, he'd know how much she longed for something deeper from him and that could send him running again, making Zephyr suffer for her foolishness.

For such a powerful, confident man, he was awfully gun-shy about being close to people. Given what she'd learned about him, she could see how he'd fear betrayal of the worst kind lurked behind the slightest show of warmth. His warnings against trying to fix him burned bright in her mind. It added up to a hopeless basis for a marriage so she felt compelled to douse any spark of that talk.

"I should answer some emails while I have the chance," she murmured, pushing herself into motion. "I won't have much chance to work through the rest of the day."

Theo watched her walk away, his tired body stirred by the graceful way she moved while the rest of him throbbed with rejection. Funny how he'd got used to women at least wanting to marry him for his money.

Not that he'd asked Jaya to marry him. He'd been careful

to phrase his question as a broad request for information, not sure why he'd brought it up when she'd said last night that she wasn't looking for money or a ring.

Still, the fact she wasn't even nibbling at the possibility of sharing her life with him was quite a slap.

But why would she want to tie herself to him? What did he offer besides money? He circled the globe every quarter, could barely change a diaper and was incapable of love. She was right to dismiss the mention of marriage.

It still left him hollow and empty.

Which was probably exaggerated by the fact he hadn't slept. As Jaya disappeared into her room, he moved to stand over the sleeping babies. They looked pretty zonked, but he couldn't take the chance of lying down on the sofa and failing to wake if they stirred. Androu was sprawled like a starfish, but Zephyr had rolled himself close to Evie.

Stealing a cushion from the sofa as a pillow, Theo settled on his side behind Zephyr then gently rested his arm across Evie's legs and settled one hand on Androu's knee. Reassured he'd hear and feel them if they woke, he let himself doze.

CHAPTER EIGHT

FEED, PLAY, CHANGE, swim, nap, change, read, play, change…
The day was eaten up quickly with the wash, rinse, spin
cycle of baby-wrangling.

"How do parents of twins manage?" he asked when Jaya
returned from taking a phone call in her room. Technically
he was on vacation, although his boss would definitely get
an earful over how relaxing this particular one had been,
but Jaya was putting out fires from downstairs at the rate
of two or three an hour while minding children at the same
time. "What if they have triplets? Or more? How do *you*
manage?"

He'd given so many horsey-rides on his ankle, he would
need a knee replacement, but Zephyr showed no sign of
tiring.

Jaya smiled. "I wasn't working when I first left Bali.
Saranya needed me and so did her daughter. Saranya tried
to hang on until I delivered, but…"

She ducked her head, taking a moment. Obviously talking about it was difficult and he had an unexpected urge to
physically reach out to her. It hurt him to see her hurting,
but he had his hands full and had never been one to act on
impulses, especially touchy-feely ones.

Still, he was sorry he couldn't somehow comfort her
when he saw how she struggled to lift a brave face.

"By the time she passed, I was so pregnant there was

no point in applying for a job. I landed this one about six months ago, but I still live with Quentin. He and I pay a neighbor to watch Bina and Zeph and spell each other off if she's not available. Quentin's been home for most of the year, doing research, so his schedule has been flexible. He'll be starting a new film soon, though. He makes documentaries and the next one will take him to South America. Bina is pressing me to go with them. Saranya and Bina always lived on location with him. I'm pleased with my life here, though, and Quentin doesn't need the money. I wish he'd stay, but he keeps saying work will take his mind off his grief." She shrugged and added in a pained tone, "They loved each other very much."

Theo had never wanted to fall in love and she'd just showcased another reason why it was a bad idea. Quentin's barely suppressed rage came back to him and he felt damned sorry for the bastard.

Nevertheless, he couldn't quit thinking about marriage.

"I'm surprised you're not plugged into the mother ship," Jaya teased, obviously trying to deflect from her own pain and lighten the mood. "I've never seen you go so long without at least one electronic device in hand."

"Haven't you?" he asked, taking a less than subtle stab at testing their shared memory. He was still raw from her rejection and wanted to remind her there had been something really good between them once. He wanted to know if this attraction was still burning as brightly on her side as it was on his.

She stalled in swiping across her tablet. Her cheeks, tanned to semi-sweet chocolate by their hour in the pool, seemed to darken. Her tongue flicked along her bottom lip in a betrayal of discomfiture that otherwise remained hidden behind her impassive expression and lowered lashes.

One of the unique things about Jaya was her subtlety. Where other women threw themselves at his money and position, she'd always seemed unimpressed. Not repelled or disgusted, but not moved, either. From things she'd said, he'd deduced that her cousin's husband had supported her to a degree, but she supported herself now and sent money to her family in India. She'd started at the bottom in Makricosta's, changing bedding and scrubbing toilets. She knew what it was to make do on a limited income, but she'd never tried to flirt or use her body to lift her circumstances or gain financial favors.

When it came to her womanly wiles, she didn't project any of her hidden depths of passion. Despite being pretty and keeping herself well-groomed, she made no effort to lure a man. Her sexuality was understated, not obvious at all.

He appreciated that about her, not because he was a man who thought women should hide their sexuality, but because he was a circumspect man all around. He admired anyone capable of controlling his or her basic, animal urges.

On the other hand, being one of the few people who knew firsthand her capacity for passion was an erotic secret that strained his control. Every time the word *marriage* whispered through his mind, the most masculine parts of him relived holding her. There'd been a couple of women since—he'd been convinced he'd never see her again and had almost been trying to inoculate himself against going after her. It hadn't worked and seeing her again was inducing the opposite: he kept imagining a lifetime of stroking smooth, warm skin, licking dark nipples that only grew more taut and firm against his tongue, pushing naked into hot, tight depths so wet and welcoming he'd nearly died on the first thrust.

"I, um, just wondered if your sister gave you the day off so you could watch her son," she finally said, not looking at him.

No outward acknowledgment of his leading comment.

He'd pretend that wasn't a sharp kick in the ego, even though they were long past pretending Bali hadn't happened. Hell, he was holding the proof.

"The cruise was supposed to be a family reunion of sorts," he explained. "Adara's idea. All the siblings were together at my mother's funeral, but it was hardly the time to catch up after not seeing Nic for twenty years. The cruise liner is a Makricosta hotel on a Vozaras ship so it would have been a working vacation, which is probably why Demitri was dragging his heels about showing up."

"He's quite the black sheep at times, isn't he?"

"And yet our father liked him. Which is why he gets away with what he does, I suppose. No one ever told him he couldn't."

"He didn't…I mean, your father never——?"

"Took a swing at him? No, I told you. Adara and I protected him. Kept him quiet when they were fighting, snuck food for him. Turned him into a spoiled brat, I suppose, but that's better than what we went through."

"You don't resent him?"

"Why would I? He was a kid. It wasn't his fault our father was a bastard."

"No," she agreed, eyes so liquid and dark he had to look away. "Only…"

Don't say it, he thought, giving all his attention to where Zephyr was now using his belly as a trampoline. Being able to see that a grown man ought to have more control over his actions than a little boy didn't make him empathetic. Being happy his brother hadn't been knocked around didn't make him paternal. It was common decency, that's all.

She came into his periphery, but only to stroke a soft hand over her son's head.

"He's having fun. Would it be an imposition to leave him with you while I do a bit more work, just while the other two are sleeping?"

An imposition? He was truly pathetic if that's how she thought he regarded holding a happy baby.

"It's fine," he said, disgusted with himself for giving off such an impression, but having a child was still a shock. And he was still so worried about damaging him he preferred to keep her close. If she wasn't hovering, how would he know he was doing everything right?

She must have read something in his tone. She glanced toward her laptop with indecision.

"Go ahead," he insisted, refusing to be frightened of a kid who couldn't even stand up on his own. "From what I've overheard, this place is still transitioning from good to excellent. You're doing a stellar job in pushing them gently, by the way. Obviously in your element. They're lucky to have you."

She checked and looked back at him. "Do you mean that?"

"Of course. I'm not surprised, either. Your knack with this kind of work was obvious to me the first time we met."

She cleared her throat. "Thank you. You're not just anyone. You know what it takes, what the pressures are. Your saying that means a lot." She gave a tiny sniff and wiped under one eye as she scooped up her laptop and moved into the bedroom.

Women. He'd like to see a male manager get all soupy from a pat on the back.

Of course, he was just as bad, still basking in her praise that he was giving his son some enjoyment. The boy had spring-loaded legs, seemingly incapable of tiring.

His son.

His chest walls gave an internal shudder as he faced a grinning countenance that seemed both foreign yet familiar. All the babies were crawling their way under his skin, but Zephyr was different. With the other two, it was easier to let himself develop some affection. There wasn't the same depth of responsibility. He imagined he'd be a fall-back for the rest of their lives, attached by bonds that nature cast like a spell for exactly this circumstance: to keep little ones alive if their primary caregiver was absent, but he wouldn't have to worry about Evie and Androu 24/7 the way he'd worry about Zephyr.

He took a moment to examine that nagging, anxious sensation. For all his concern that he'd crush this boy's confidence, the what-ifs about his future were worse. What if he was wet and this neighbor lady didn't notice? What if Quentin talked Jaya into taking the boy to some third-world country with exotic parasites and deadly spiders? What if something happened to Jaya?

The way Zephyr chewed a finger and thumb while staring deeply into his eyes—much the same disconcerting way his mother had, as if he trusted him implicitly—was a heart punch. It was as if the little guy was already relying on Theo to make sure all the what-ifs were mitigated. Who else would do it? Theo had a lot of faults, but shirking responsibility was not one of them.

His guts wobbled, like he'd taken a misstep on a high wire.

No, he didn't shirk responsibility. If Jaya had said *that* to him last night, rather than trying to prod him into admitting an emotional connection to the boy, she might have had him.

But who *would* look after Zephyr if something happened to Jaya? He'd seen what babies were like when Mama wasn't near. They were distressed. He wouldn't want Zephyr to go through that. Hell, *he* didn't want to go through missing Jaya again and he was a full-grown man.

Swearing under his breath, he tried to take back that thought, but it was acknowledged now. Was that why he was stressing out about Zephyr's future, he asked himself? Because the tyke was his best excuse to hang on to the mother?

No. He did not just see Zephyr as a means to an end. When he contemplated walking away from Jaya *or* Zephyr, everything in him went bleak and gray. His sense of responsibility toward the boy was quickly shifting beyond the desire to provide food and shelter. Quentin might be the better father figure, but Theo couldn't shake Jaya's comment that maybe he'd never developed any deep relationships because he didn't cultivate them.

It wasn't fair to Zephyr to not even *try,* was it?

Zephyr stopped bouncing and gave an exhausted sigh, like he'd finished chopping a cord of wood. Theo found himself grinning in amusement.

"Finally worn out?" He settled the boy against his chest where Zephyr let his head droop, fingers still in his mouth and eyelids heavy.

He wasn't a man who cuddled, preferring his own space unless he was busy with a woman between the sheets, but there was an addictive quality to a baby's snuggled warmth against his shoulder. It was a sense of all-powerfulness. Success at creating a moment of contentment for another human being. After a childhood of being found wanting, he wallowed in Zephyr's unconditional appreciation of having his simplest needs met.

It's just Mother Nature's plan, he tried to dismiss, but a very tiny voice—feminine and lilting with an Indian accent—whispered that maybe it was a father's nature to be happy when his child was happy.

Stunned, he swallowed a lump of emotion, hands cradling his son tenderly as the connection between them wound through him like a creeping vine, hooking into his vital organs in such a way there'd be damage to both of them if they were pulled apart.

Jaya's quiet voice grew louder, speaking to Evie as she appeared with the girl. Her eyes went soft when she saw him holding Zephyr so close, making Theo feel as though he was out on that high wire again, a brisk gale cutting up the canyon toward him.

He lowered his gaze. This was too personal a moment to have even Jaya witness.

"Trade?" he asked in a voice like sandpaper, reluctant to let the boy go, but he was so shaken by his flood of primal instinct to protect and nurture, he let her steal the sleepy baby and tried to distract himself by coaxing a smile from Evie with a promise of a swim later.

It was soon back to chaos, Androu waking shortly after Evie and both of them hungry. He was washing mashed banana out of Androu's hair, using the wet cloth to spike it into a Mohawk, wondering if he was getting the hang of this parenting thing after all, when a knock at the door interrupted them.

Jaya was in her room, answering emails while Zephyr napped in there with her. He sidled to the peephole and saw Nic, Rowan and Adara distorted by the fisheye lens.

Never one to appreciate unexpected visitors, he snapped open the door. "Why didn't you call?"

"Are they okay? Where are they?" The women rushed past him like fans into a rock concert, invading his space.

Nic entered at a more laconic pace, scanning the suite in the way of someone who made his living by sharp observations.

Theo suppressed a prickle of irritability. The place was littered in toys and dirty dishes. Much as he didn't really care about being judged over something like that, he also made it a habit to keep from providing opportunities to be judged.

"They were anxious so I chartered a helicopter," Nic said. "Gideon had to stay with the ship. Everyone is okay, but what a mess. I don't envy him. There's my girl." He broke into a wide smile as he caught Evie reaching from Rowan's arms into his.

"It's not that we didn't trust you, Theo. We just missed them so much," Rowan said, her light touch on his arm apologetic.

He gave a jerky shrug, subtly removing himself from her uninvited touch even though he didn't hate it. She was nice enough and being sincere. It was just he wasn't at his best, accosted by a lot right now with their unexpected visit and a distant, illogical disappointment he didn't want to examine. He didn't need her standing too close, sensing his tension, reading his vibe for him.

"It's fine, I understand," he said, and strangely, kind of did. His chest filled with pressure at the way his sister was smothering the life out of Androu. Her eyes were closed, her lashes wet. He had a new understanding of how precious their babies were to them and was suffused with a weird self-conscious pride that he'd been able to keep their offspring safe for them, whether they had really trusted him to do so or not.

"I knew he'd be fine. He knows you," Adara said, voice thick. "But Gideon threw you into the deep end with both of them. I'm glad you called Jaya—she's perfect—but what made you think of her? How did you know she was here? Where *is* she?"

Before Theo could get past the suffocation provoked by questions about Jaya, she said, "I'm here."

They all turned toward her voice.

"Sorry," she said with a flash of anxious eyes at Theo. "The commotion woke him and he needs a drink."

Zephyr looked sweaty and flushed, hair damp and pushed up in tufts around the face he buried in Jaya's neck to hide.

Theo moved to fetch the boy's cup, distancing himself from something he didn't want to face, then kicked himself just as quickly. This was exactly the kind of abandonment he would hate himself for inflicting on his son. Or Jaya, for that matter.

"I'm sorry we spoiled his nap," he heard Rowan say and glanced across to see her peeking at the boy over his mother's shoulder. "What's your name?"

"Baby Zepper," Evie provided from her happy perch on Nic's bent arm.

"Zephyr," Jaya corrected softly, smiling at Evie. "You've been my best little helper, haven't you? She's been very sweet with both of them."

"Zephyr," Rowan repeated. "That's lovely. Greek god of wind, right?"

Theo absorbed the meaning, wondering if it was a deliberate reference to his love of piloting, thinking, *I really don't deserve her,* as he crossed with Zephyr's sipping cup.

"Thanks," Jaya said with a flickering gaze of apprehension as he approached. She rubbed Zephyr's back to get his attention. "Want your cup, sweetie?"

Zephyr lifted his head and spied the cup, but rather than wait for Jaya to take it, he leaned out for Theo.

Theo was getting used to the boy's impulsive launches. He caught him in what was becoming a practiced scoop and hitched him up against his chest. The air in his lungs stopped moving as he held the cup for the boy, aware of how telling his actions were, how much like a father he must appear. How close a copy of Androu Zephyr was.

Zephyr's little hands settled over his big one while profound silence fell over the room like a dome.

Theo forced himself to lift his gaze and meet each pair of stunned eyes. They had to be reading guilt in him. It sprang from ignoring Jaya's attempts to contact him and thinking he could ignore someone as important as his son. He was ashamed of himself, not Zephyr.

Disgust with himself made him blurt, "He's mine," aware that it was the clumsiest possible way he could have announced it, but he couldn't dance around it. Not when Nic was drilling him a look that said, *You lucky bastard.*

His half brother blinked and the envy was gone, replaced by a doting smile at Evie, but it was the reinforcement Theo needed to keep inching across the hot coals cooking him from the soles of his feet to his collar. Maybe he wasn't doing this well, but he'd figured out what was right and he'd do that much.

In his periphery, he saw Jaya lift an uncertain hand then fold her arms defensively. *Don't,* he wanted to say. *Don't be embarrassed for me. I don't care how stupid I look, only that I not fail where it counts.*

Over Zephyr's loud gulps, Androu made a noise and put out his hand.

"I told you before, sport," Theo said, trying to sound normal while emotions log-jammed in his throat. "Yours is the green one. It's on his tray," he told Adara, nodding to the high chair where Androu had been sitting before she arrived.

He hoped she'd move away and begin to defuse this charged moment, but she didn't. Her gaze was fixed on Zephyr's face.

The boy looked at her with his unblinking brown eyes. Makricosta eyes.

"Theo." She spoke his name with myriad inflections. Shock, awe, surprise, approval. Exasperated *dis*approval.

As he braced himself for whatever she would say, he felt a feminine hand rest on his biceps. Jaya. If he'd had a free hand, he would have wrapped it around her waist and pulled her in close. He might be willing to face the scrutiny of his family without apology, but it wasn't easy. How such a slight woman could be his shield against them, he didn't understand, but he had an intense need to wield her in just that way.

"He didn't know," Jaya said. The tips of her fingers dug into his tense arm. "Not until I told him yesterday."

Had it only been a day?

He drew in a breath, realizing he'd neglected to take in air for several seconds. Looking into Jaya's eyes, he let her know she didn't have to protect him *that* much. It was his own damned fault he hadn't known about his son.

It's okay, she seemed to reassure with a softening of her touch on his arm. *Our secret.* And therein lay her appeal. He feared every stumble, too used to being knocked down a second time for daring to err. She was a forgiving person, though. She was so softhearted, she'd help him to his feet after a face-plant. He wanted to kiss her for it.

Hell, he wanted to kiss her, period. He dragged himself free of their locked stare in time to hear Rowan ask Nic, "Will it be a full Indian wedding, do you think? I've always wanted to go to one."

Jaya's touch on his arm fell away.

Theo stiffened, struck anew by rejection.

"I'm making assumptions, aren't I?" Rowan said with a blush and a reach for her daughter. "Come on, Evie, let's find Androu's cup for him."

"I'll help," Nic said, taking Androu as he passed Adara. "Drink, champ?"

Jaya watched the Viking blond media mogul and his petite wife distance themselves toward the kitchen, leaving Adara staring at their ill at ease vignette.

Zephyr was comfortable enough, she supposed, taking a break from draining his cup to huff a breath and stare after his cousins, but she was hyper-conscious of Theo statue-stiff next to her.

"Will he come to me?" Adara asked, approaching with hands raised.

Her intense focus, the way she caught her breath as Zephyr went to her, the way she enfolded him and pressed her smile into his hair, all made Jaya want to turn her crinkling forehead into Theo's chest.

Having Zephyr accepted by Theo's sister was beyond her dreams. She wished she'd known it would go this well or she might have tried harder to reach him. She might have gone directly to Adara.

"I should have—" Jaya began.

"Don't." He caught her wrist. "*I* should have," he said, as if he knew what she'd been about to say. His hand slid to mesh with hers, palm to palm, fingers entwined.

It was such a startling gesture she could only cling to him, at sea as to how to react. He'd surprised her by claiming Zephyr so openly when she'd been expecting to be treated like a dirty little secret. Having him hold her hand as if there was something between them besides a baby was a kind of magic she knew she shouldn't believe in, but she wanted to.

"I never thought I'd hold your baby," Adara said with a misty smile. "I hoped Androu would rub off on you, but— Wait a minute. How old is he?" She pulled back to study the boy, eyes narrow as she lifted them to Theo's culpable swallow.

"It was—" Jaya started to excuse, but Theo squeezed her hand. Her entire being was warmed by his firm grip, radiating heat up her arm and into her chest.

"I'm not going to offer excuses—or details. Fire me if you have to," Theo said.

Adara gave him a look between stern and maddened. "I'll assume that if you deserved to be fired, you'd say so. Demitri is the one that needs reminders about employees being off-limits. Besides, I can't be mad. We have a nephew. Gideon will be over the moon." She smiled at Zephyr as the boy reached for Jaya, letting him go.

Jaya had to pull her hand free of Theo's to take Zephyr and secure him on her hip.

In the carefully emotionless way that Jaya was more familiar seeing in Adara she heard her ask Theo, "What *are* your plans?"

In the blink of one glance, a lot of teeming undercurrents were exchanged between brother and sister. It niggled at Jaya in a way she couldn't interpret. They seemed almost telepathic and it made her feel left out.

She imagined there were considerations with regards to the Makricosta fortune, though. Publicity to finesse and old-fashioned concern for family. Given Theo's dismay at learning he was a father, she expected him to request Zephyr's existence be kept quiet.

With an impactful look at Jaya, Theo became super tall, his posture and air very authoritative. She'd seen him take a hard line when it came to accounting rules, but had never seen him turn such an uncompromising look on her.

"I don't want to miss any more of Zephyr's life than I have," he said.

Oh. Jaya's heart fluttered, surprised by this evolution in his attitude. He'd been tentative yesterday, but she supposed that had been shock. This morning he'd seemed to accept he had a son, even if it had still been a perplexing addition to his life.

Now she could see acknowledgment had moved into something more implacable that was both heartening and threatening. It had never occurred to her that she might have to fight him for her child, but she saw something in his eyes that was resolute and possessive. Something that told her Zephyr had taken up residence inside him in a way she'd been dreaming of doing since Day One.

Why did that make her jealous? She ought to be happy.

"We haven't agreed on how we're moving forward," Theo continued. "But whether it's a big wedding or not— I'll be pushing for marriage."

CHAPTER NINE

THE WORDS CAME between them in an eclipse-like flash. For a second Jaya couldn't breathe, couldn't see.

No. She'd already told him no. Hadn't he heard her? But what she'd really been refusing was a marriage of convenience. If he loved her... Did he?

And how could he just announce it like that to his sister without consulting—without even *asking* her first?

"I haven't convinced Jaya yet," Theo said, taking the weight of his penetrating stare back to his sister.

Oh, sure, put it all on me, Jaya thought, working to keep a scowl off her face. Her instinct was to protest, but she didn't want to draw Adara into it. Given the look exchanged between Nic and Rowan as they returned from the kitchen, they'd heard Theo, adding to her feeling of being outnumbered.

No one needed to know her reasons for refusing to marry except maybe Theo and she'd share that only if and when it felt right.

"We haven't had much time to talk about anything except whose turn it is to change a bottom," Jaya murmured, stroking a hand over Androu's tousled hair as he toddled after Evie to their play area in the lounge.

"Understood," Nic said. "And we're incredibly grateful for your help. If you ever need anything, please let us know."

"I expect we'll be seeing a lot of each other regardless," Rowan said with a warm smile. "Evie's forever begging for Androu and seems equally rapt with Zephyr. I expect a few tears when we leave, to be honest. Brace yourself. She has a tender little heart."

It was true. After thirty minutes of letting the children have a last play together while the adults gathered up toys and clothes, they congregated at the door. Evie broke into pieces when she realized the other children wouldn't be coming with her to Greece.

"Peas, Papa," she begged through her tears.

"I'm sorry, but they have to live with their own mamas."

She wasn't trying to manipulate; she was genuinely heartbroken, weeping into his shoulder with loss.

Her suffering twisted Jaya's heart so badly she found herself promising to bring Zephyr for a visit.

After a tearful kiss and hug from the girl, she said goodbye and was emotionally wrung out as she and Theo moved into the quiet lounge.

"Did I just promise a two-year-old I'd fly to Greece to see her?" Jaya collapsed into a chair. "I can't afford that."

Theo gave her a dry, are-you-kidding look. "Nic has his own plane and so do I." He leaned back on the sofa, hands behind his head, gaze lifting from where Zephyr sat on the floor rattling the stuffing out of a toy bear. "I'll take you as soon as we work out a convenient time."

Her heart lifted while her stomach swooped. The word *honeymoon* blinked like a lighthouse flash in her mind, but she turned away from it. She stared at their baby rather than looking at Theo, nervous of the masculine energy he was projecting. He might appear relaxed, but they were alone now, the buffer of activity gone. The full force of his male magnetism was blasting into her, stronger than she remembered it.

"You're assuming a lot," she said, leaning forward to

remove a hard toy from behind Zephyr. "I'm not quitting my job. I'm not marrying you."

Silence, then, "I realize I threw that at you from left field."

"You did," she snapped. "That wasn't fair."

"I didn't mean to, but…" He sat forward, swearing as he rubbed his face. "Both Adara and Rowan had fertility issues. I could see Nic was thinking anyone who would turn away from the chance to be a father—"

"Are you seriously saying that the only reason you want to be in Zephyr's life is to avoid being judged by your family?" She *lived* that hell, but it was because she was determined to stay true to herself. For him to buckle to their expectations was a very dishonest start to his relationship with Zephyr, something she wouldn't tolerate no matter the consequences.

"No, it reinforced to me what a gift he is. Not everyone has the luxury of one night producing a baby. Yes, this has been hard for me to come to terms with." He waved a confounded hand at their son, but a subtle tenderness crept beneath his hard visage as he watched Zephyr discover his own toes and try to catch them in his waving hand. "I'm still not convinced I'm father material, but Nic figured it out. Maybe I've got a shot. And if there's one thing my childhood taught me, it's how to avoid making mistakes, especially big ones. Turning my back on my son would be a terrible one."

He was saying all the right things, but rather than creating a sense of relief in her, he was undermining her defenses. She needed resentment to keep her from tumbling back into the depths of her crazy crush on him. That sort of weakness would complicate things. She'd start thinking about what she wanted, rather than what she and Zephyr needed.

"We still don't have to marry," she mumbled.

"What would living together do to your relationship with your family?"

"You want to live together?" The words dissolved everything around her so nothing had substance. She was falling, unable to grasp anything that would ground her.

"Yesterday you pointed out that I don't stick around to develop relationships. It's true. If I want to know my son, I have to be near him. Physically." He frowned as he said it, like he wasn't sure, but would give it a try.

That's all she needed, to let him become a daily part of her life then have him quit on her. "I don't want to live with you," she insisted.

"Why not? You live with Quentin. I'll pay for everything."

Back to money. Was there a problem in his world that he wouldn't try to buy his way out of?

"I value my independence," she said.

"But you're not independent," he countered. "You have a son. You and I are connected through him and that makes us interdependent." He pointed between them, as if running lines of webbing that stitched them together. He didn't seem any happier about it than she was. "We have to compromise for his best interest. We'll have to do that for the rest of our lives. There's no getting around that."

Hurt that he was only trying to make a life with her because he thought it was the ethical thing to do, she rose to pace, winding up facing a window, arms folded.

"I grew up fighting tooth and nail for every decision I wanted to make for myself. I won't have the same fight with you. I won't give up and do as I'm told. You're making me feel like I have to live with you. That I have to marry you. I already live with a lot of have-to's as a result of my choosing to have Zephyr."

"You think I don't know how it feels to live under someone else's rules?" he countered. "You think I enjoy calculating interest rates and double-checking the inventory of hand towels? There's a difference between being subjugated and placing duty to family above self-interest. My father isn't around to disinherit me if I quit my job. I stay for Adara's sake, because I want her to succeed. Although we'll have to make adjustments to my duties if I'm going to spend any time with you and Zephyr."

He muffled a curse behind his hand, glowering while his gaze turned inward.

Her stomach did a flip flop, latching too tightly onto his *with you.* She shook it off, not wanting to be so easily drawn in by him. Turning, she considered the dual notes of frustration and sincerity in his voice.

"You hate your job?" she prompted.

He quirked the tight line of his lips before saying, "Don't tell Adara." He shrugged that off. "I don't really hate it, not anymore, but it's not what I would have chosen for myself. My father pushed me into it. He would have taken it out on Adara if I'd rebelled so I kept the peace and took an Econ degree. The work is more enjoyable now that she trusts my numbers and makes the kinds of decisions we always knew were the better ones. We actually see the profits we're looking for. I was constantly set up for failure while my father was alive. That was hell."

She came back to sit across from him. Linking her hands, she pressed her knuckles to her mouth. "I think I hate your father," she admitted in a muted voice. The man bore a lot of blame for Theo's inability to give her what she wanted from him.

"Join the club," he retorted, then expelled a tired breath. "But he's gone so do what I do. Forget him."

Releasing her inner lip from the bite of her teeth, she added, "He is gone, so don't turn me into something you think you have to do. You have a choice, too, Theo."

"I do," he agreed and hitched forward on the edge of the

sofa. "That's what I'm saying. I'm not acting from a sense of duty, although I feel a pretty strong one toward both of you. It's a different kind of 'have to.' The kind that means I wouldn't be able to live with myself if I didn't do what's right by the two of you."

Which framed her refusal to marry him as inexcusable selfishness.

"I can appreciate that you want to be part of Zephyr's life." She couldn't countenance anything less herself. "But live together? Like as roommates?"

"If that's what you prefer." He blinked once, keeping his expression neutral so she couldn't tell what he really thought of the arrangement.

"For how long? Until he's in school? Until he's grown? And what are you doing all this time? Bringing women home?"

"No," he dismissed flatly and cast a gaze toward the pool, one that was stark and seemed rather isolated and lonely.

Her heart shook. She willed it to still, not wanting to be affected. *Don't try to fix him.*

"Is there nothing on your side, Jaya? Of what we had before?" he asked quietly.

She caught her breath, plunged into the deep end, sinking and sinking, pressure gathering in her ears and pressing outward in her lungs. Her vision blurred because she forgot to blink.

"What did we have?" she asked in a thin voice, reminding herself that neither of them had been seeking a long term relationship that night. Her motives had been, if not emotionless, at least not as simple as his.

"More chemistry than I've ever felt for anyone else, before or since." His blunt words detonated a terrific blush in her, making her cover her hot cheeks and look anywhere but at him.

"I didn't mean to behave that way," she moaned, still embarrassed that once hadn't been enough. Twice had been decadent self-indulgence. The third time had been outright greed, stolen against the hands of the clock.

"I loved how you behaved," he said, voice low and taut with sweet memory.

Her heart tripped as he began speaking and stumbled into the dust as she realized it wasn't a declaration of deep feeling. She was still affected, still transported back to a night when touching a man had seemed the most natural, perfect thing in the world to do.

The glint of masculine interest in his eye sparked a depth of need in her she had worried she'd never feel again.

"Okay, then," he said in a satisfied growl, his fixed gaze weighted with lazy approval.

"Theo, don't!" She pushed the heels of her hands into her eyes. Her history with him, especially their night together, had stolen a lot of power from her darkest memories, but, "Don't make assumptions about me and sex. Please. Saying I'm attracted to you doesn't mean I want to have sex with you. It's not that simple for me. Ever."

"Hey, I'm not taking anything for granted," he admonished. "I realize sex could be a hindrance to our working out a good long-term solution. Much as I want to have an affair with you, if we burn out it would have consequences for Zephyr. I get that."

Did he? Because she hadn't got that far. All she could think was that she hadn't expected to have another shot at sharing Theo's bed and really didn't know how she felt about climbing into it again, especially long-term. Talk about assumptions. That would create a lot. All her conflicting yes-no signals were firing, making her cautious even as she found herself literally warming to the idea.

"But you have to admit, we're a good team, Jaya. That's all Adara and Gideon had going for them when they married. Maybe they had sexual attraction, I don't know. I would never ask," he said with a dismissing sweep of his hand and an expression of juvenile repugnance that would have been laughable if her thoughts weren't exploding like popcorn kernels in oil.

"You and I have as good a base as they had," he insisted. "Maybe a better one. We know each other a lot better than they did. An affair, living together… Those are too easy to walk away from. Marriage would force us to work out whatever differences came up. Zephyr needs that kind of stability and commitment. Doesn't he?"

Here was the clarity he'd told her he was capable of. He could see the right course of action even if he didn't know whether he could perform it. Even when he wasn't terribly keen to embrace it.

Still, she was half persuaded by his rationale. He was right and talking about it like they were negotiating a merger kept her from being swept away, allowing her to view the situation objectively.

That's what she told herself anyway, to counter the thick knot of disappointment sitting in her throat.

"Are you hesitating because of what I told you about my father? You're worried I'll resort to abuse?"

"No!" she blurted, heartfelt and sincere. Her waffling feelings were more about having her heart suffer from un-requited attraction than worrying about physical harm.

"If that's what's worrying you, admit it. I'll forget the whole thing. I totally understand." He stood and caught up Zephyr, repositioning him in the middle of the blanket, his movements hiding his face, but she thought she caught a glint of profound hurt. Maybe something else. A sort of hopeless defeat.

"Theo, I don't think you could hurt me or Zephyr even if you wanted to. If we needed a snakebite carved out of us, you probably couldn't do it."

His glance flickered toward her in acknowledgment, colored with ironic humor, but he moved to stand looking through the glass at the pool. He pushed his hands into his pockets, shoulders slumped.

"You've been so willing to listen to everything I've told you I let myself believe it didn't matter, but of course it matters. Of course you have to take time to consider what it means and decide whether you can trust me."

She was going to have to tell him. She could see his back tensed against the same kind of betrayal and injury he'd already suffered. She couldn't leave him thinking something as far out of his control as his childhood abuse would cause her to fear him.

Still, her abdomen tightened as if clenching to accept a blow.

"Theo, it's not you, it's me."

He barked out a laugh and sent an askance look over his shoulder. "Okay."

Not in front of Zephyr, she thought, but their son had tipped onto his side and was contentedly chewing a finger and pedaling his feet. And wasn't he the manifestation of the goodness that had come out of her bad experience? If she hadn't been assaulted, she would have stayed in India and married under her uncle's dictate. Instead, she'd left and wound up meeting Theo and he had changed her life profoundly, giving her this gift.

"I trust you, Theo. I wouldn't have slept with you in Bali if I didn't."

"That's different. One night is not a lifetime. A pair of lost souls finding comfort in physical pleasure is not marriage. It takes a lot more faith in a person to share every aspect of your life with him. I understand."

"No, that's not—" She sighed. "That's not what Bali was for me. Not all it was."

He came around a half step, body still in profile, his grave expression watchful. "What do you mean?"

She took a shaky breath. "The reason I left India…" She pinched her lip, trying to stay focused. "I should back up to explain. I've told you Saranya and I grew up very close? When I was six, my father had an accident on the tractor and was forced to sign our land over to my uncle. We moved in with them. Our mothers are twins. It's a big house, not a bad arrangement except that my uncle is quite controlling. He has very traditional views where women are concerned."

She set the jungle gym over Zephyr so he could swat at the dangling toys.

"Saranya grew up dreaming of being in Bollywood films. Uncle was fit to be tied. He was arranging a marriage for her when Quentin's crew came into the next village. Saranya was convinced this was her break. In a way it was. They fell in love and she eloped with him."

"And you were left with her angry, thwarted father."

She nodded. "And her two brothers and my younger brother and sister. Uncle became more domineering than ever, dictating to my parents how we should behave. It was one of the reasons I was so resolved to get a job, to give my parents money so they wouldn't be so dependent on him. He objected to me working, saying I should marry, but there were other young people going into call centers, bringing money home. A friend recommended me for a position and it was good work. I improved my English, used their lines to speak with Saranya," she confessed with a sheepish grin. "Uncle had disowned her, but I missed her."

"Are you trying to tell me you're afraid I won't let you work?"

"There is that, but no, that's not where I'm going." Rising to try to escape the cloying sense of helplessness that still managed to smother her at times, she paced across the room then halted, arms wrapped around herself.

What would he think of her? Would he blame her as her family had?

"The problem with my job was... There was a man there. My supervisor. He was older, in his forties. I wasn't even twenty yet. He flirted with me, but it wasn't flirting."

"Sexual harassment," Theo concluded flatly, his voice low and chill.

"One night, before I went home, it was sexual assault." Her voice faded into a whisper, but she knew he heard her because the silence took on a thick, heavy quality.

She smoothed a hand over the glossy hardwood of a side table, accidentally lifting her eyes to the reflection in the mirror above it.

Theo was arrested, pale under his swarthy tan, lips tight and outlined with a white ring. When their gazes clashed in the pool of silver, he flinched his glance away.

She caught back a gasp of pain.

"I never should have pressured you that night," he said from between his teeth.

"You didn't. I wanted to," she assured him, swinging around to face him even though her whole body suffused with self-conscious heat. Memories burned through her, sweet and hot. Hands knotting together at her navel, she said in a strained voice, "You know I enjoyed it."

She was dying over here, embarrassed that she had to be so bald in her confession. It was incredibly hard to practically beg him to remember how uninhibited she'd been by the time she'd slipped naked from his bed and reluctantly dressed, but she had faced him proudly in the dawn light, enjoying his admiring gaze as he watched her dress.

"That night was the first time since it happened that I wanted to be with a man. To let anyone touch me," she confided.

"I was your employer."

"No, you weren't. And remember how shocked I was

that you were attracted to me? As an employee I never once felt threatened by you, especially sexually. I was as grateful for that as everything else. I mean, I started out in house-keeping because it was all women, even the supervisors. Moving to the front desk, night clerk, those were all huge risks that I took because I knew I had to move past what had happened to me if I wanted to advance, but I was able to do it because you had this quiet command of everything. I felt like no one would dare touch me because I could go to you. I didn't have any recourse the first time."

He frowned. "You didn't tell your family? What about the police?"

Thick painful tears welled in her eyes and she had to look away to hold on to her composure. "My uncle was ashamed that I went to the police. He called me a slut and my parents weren't in a position to argue in my defense. They wanted me to marry the man, but he was already married."

Theo swore and started toward her only to bring himself up short. "Jaya…" His tone was one of deep shock and struggle.

She wished he'd make this easy and take her in his strong arms, but at the same time she could only stare at the floor feeling the tears drop from her eyes. The assault had been a nightmare, but the time afterward had been the darkest, most bleak and isolated of her life.

Forcing herself to remember it was over and she was safe, she swiped at her wet cheeks and lifted her head, lashes matted and eyes still bleary. Swallowing back the lump in her throat, she managed to say, "Fortunately I had Saranya."

"She came for you?"

"Couriered her passport. My uncle had learned his lesson about leaving them where the children could find them. We're only a year apart and always looked remarkably

alike. People mistook us all the time. Quentin was filming in Malaysia so she sent me a ticket to Kuala Lumpur.
She'd just had Bina. They took me in and she went with me
for all the doctor checks… I look back and think it's such
a miracle I didn't get pregnant, given you and I managed
it in one go." She gave a weak smile.

"I can't believe you still send them money."

"For my mother's sake, and my sister's. And even though
Quentin is quite successful, I don't want to be a burden.
I lived too long on my uncle's good graces. Earning my
own keep is important to me so I applied at a few hotels, ones that overlooked my lack of paperwork. Having
good English was an asset. I picked up Quentin's German
and a local dialect. When he began filming in Bali, I got
on at Makricosta's. After, um, claiming to the Indian em-
bassy that I'd lost my passport and needed it replaced." She
cleared her throat. "I know that was wrong—"

"Hell, Jaya, I'm not judging you. Your uncle, yeah, but
not you." He swore again and ran a hand down his face.

Zephyr squawked at that point and she realized he was
probably hungry. It was a much-needed few minutes of
distraction that allowed her to collect herself. Her hands
shook as she moved around the kitchenette and she was
aware of Theo standing in one spot the whole time, staring out to the pool.

The sense of being flayed raw stayed with her, making her attempts to be natural and smile at her baby feel
forced. Her cheeks were stiff, her brow hooking and pulling. Everything in her wanted to move into Theo's reach
and hope he'd take her in his arms, so he might smooth
away all the jagged edges and reassure her that what she'd
told him hadn't changed his view of her.

He didn't even look her way, which choked her throat
with a helpless ache.

The buzz of her phone, which was on vibrate, jangled

her nerves. She thought, *Work,* and it was the most vile four-letter word right now.

Except it would also be a healthy retreat. It suddenly hit her that she *could* leave. Theo didn't need her here. The babies were gone.

Oh. An even more profoundly bereft emotion enveloped her, but she needed distance from him. While her emotions were twining and growing around his return to her life, she couldn't tell what he was thinking. That marriage idea of his certainly wasn't being thrown at her any longer.

Against the ominous plane of his back, she said, "I'll take Zephyr home after he finishes eating. A lot has piled up here. I need to get into my office downstairs."

Theo turned and the withdrawal in him was almost frightening. He was the aloof man she'd first met, not dismissive, but giving the impression he didn't see a woman at all. Just a fellow robot.

The shift crushed her with disappointment. No, something worse. She was devastated. It was like all the accord they'd developed had evaporated and she was a stranger to him. He would be polite, but really, he didn't want to know her ugly secrets. She'd told him too much and now she felt small and soiled.

"Why don't you leave him with me?" he said.

"Wh-what?"

"I'm not going anywhere. We'll be close by if he needs you. You and I still have to figure out how we're going to proceed. I've heard all you've said, I understand why you don't want to marry me, but I'm not flying out of here to forget this ever happened. At some point word will get out beyond my siblings that I have a child. He's every bit as vulnerable as Evie and Androu, security-wise. We have a lot to work out."

He spoke from across the canyon that was the lounge, his words seeming to echo around her, but they weren't quite as empty as she'd begun to fear. She stood on uncertain footing, but this connection he'd talked about, their interdependence, was real. It was a thin thread, delicate as a dew-covered string of spider silk, but she stayed very still, wanting it to stick and endure.

"Okay." She had to clear huskiness from her throat and now her smile at Zephyr was soft and easy and relieved. She felt like she could breathe again. *She would keep seeing Theo a little longer.*

"If you don't mind a late dinner, we could talk then," she offered as she wiped Zephyr's face and hands.

"Downstairs? That's fine. What time shall I make the reservation?"

She had meant room service, but, "I can book it. I'll text you." Feeling gauche and self-conscious, she walked Zephyr across to Theo's tense presence and escaped to gather her composure.

Theo closed his eyes as the door shut behind Jaya.

It wasn't fair to look to an infant for comfort, but he snugged the boy close against him and pressed his unsteady lips against hair dark and silky smooth as his mother's.

The surge of emotions in him was almost too much to bear, certainly near impossible to contain while Jaya had been in the room. Lovely Jaya who wouldn't crush a spider, brutalized by a man she'd trusted. He hadn't had the courage to ask for details. They only mattered if she felt a need to get them off her chest. He certainly didn't want to hear them. As far as he was concerned, the fact it had happened at all was infuriating and heartbreaking enough, but to then not even be supported by her family...

It was unthinkable, blasting him to overflowing with a need to insist—demand—that she marry him and be forevermore under his protection. He wasn't superhuman, but he had resources the average person couldn't touch. The proverbial shields he could place around her were near bullet-proof and his blood raced with the need to affix them. Now.

But she didn't want to rely on him, didn't want to marry him.

If her assailant had reached into his chest and clawed out his heart he couldn't have stolen anything more vital to him than Jaya's trust. Theo had suggested they eat in the public dining room because he was convinced she wouldn't want to be alone with him, and she'd agreed. What did that say?

And here he'd been fantasizing—not taking for granted, only indulging himself—that the sexual attraction was still ripe and strong between them. That it could form the basis of a marriage that stood half a chance.

His fury at the injustice made him want to scream, but he had a child in his arms. A tiny boy who had somehow come to life after Jaya had suffered one of the worst types of betrayal.

He brought the boy up so they were eye to eye. Zephyr's wide grin caused a crack to zigzag across his heart. Not one of damage, but as if the shell that encased it was breaking open. Tender hunger for more of those smiles, more time with Jaya, leaked out.

Never one to believe the Christmas present he wanted would actually be under the tree, he still let a nascent thought form: Maybe if he was very careful with her, there would be hope.

CHAPTER TEN

WHEN JAYA WAS called to the front desk because Bina was asking for her there, her first instinct was to send her cousin home. Quentin had sent the girl with her sitter to check up on her, acting like an interfering, if somewhat endearing, overbearing male relative.

But Bina had a genuine connection to Zephyr that helped the girl cope with the loss she was still grieving. Jaya didn't have the heart to send her away without a visit with her cherished baby cousin. Plus, an uninterrupted conversation with Theo for the first time since she'd seen him again held a lot of appeal.

She texted him that Bina and her nanny were coming up to stay with Zephyr and she'd meet him at the bell desk to go for dinner. Then, in a minor fit of vanity, she visited one of the hotel's boutiques, using her employee discount to buy a new dress and shoes.

Studying herself in the mirror of the staff washroom, she asked herself what she was trying to prove. Her hair was brushed, her makeup refreshed. The only pair of shoes she could find to go with this dress were much taller than she'd normally wear. They had bling. A line of sequins decorated the heel and a jazzy buckle drew attention to the toes Bina had painted a neon pink when they'd been having girls' night a week ago.

The dress was more feminine than sexy with its ruffled

layers of sheer red and orange and pink and fluttering split cut sleeves, but gave her a moment of sober second thought.

She refused to dress like a frump, though. Her confession this afternoon had been difficult. Part of her wanted to crawl into a cave now that her secret was revealed, but she knew better than to let her past cow her. She wouldn't deny the fact she was a woman. She wouldn't pretend to be ugly or asexual. That would only feed her shame and she had nothing to be ashamed of. Being pretty wasn't a crime. Wanting to please the eye of a man wasn't a broad invitation to be abused by all of them.

Still, it was an act of bravery to swipe a final layer of gloss onto her lips and take herself to the bell desk. The bellman was engaged and only Theo stood there.

He stared broodingly at the bobbing lights against the dark backdrop of water beyond the windows, his demeanor the quietly compelling man she'd so admired from afar in Bali. Pausing, she allowed herself a few seconds to take in his profile of statue stillness. He projected casual wealth with his gold watch and tailored shirt over crisp pants with their break in the cuff where they landed on his Italian loafers. Since he took these things for granted, he emanated power. And he was so *attractive* with his fit body and neat haircut and perfectly hewn, freshly shaved jaw.

She had always thought he had it all, had so much he was bored with the world, but she knew him so much better now. He held himself remote as a self-protective thing and that made her see him with new eyes. She realized he must be terribly lonely.

He glanced abstractly toward her, then started with a flash of surprised recognition. Maybe something else. She wasn't sure what she saw between his raking gaze from her lashes to her fancy shoes. He quickly masked his expression.

"No uniform," he commented.

No compliment, either.

"I didn't want to start any rumors if the Makricosta CFO was recognized having dinner with our general manager. I made reservations across the road."

He nodded without reaction and held the door for her as they walked across to *La Fumée Blanche,* The White Mist. She'd secretly wanted to try the dinner and dance restaurant forever, but it was a place for couples, not singles or a woman and her preadolescent niece.

They were shown through a dining room surrounding a small dance floor. On a dais, a trio played French jazz, filling the room with the Pink Panther sound of a brush against a cymbal. Their table had fresh roses, plush velvet chairs and a spectacular view of the Med.

It would have been perfect if she didn't feel like Theo was wearing his CFO hat and picturing her in her Makricosta blouse.

"Wine?" he asked.

"I thought you don't drink?"

"I thought you might."

"Sometimes." She flushed at how awkward this was. Maybe they needed Zephyr between them after all. "If it's a special occasion, but I don't need anything tonight."

This wasn't special, even though the candle glinted flecks of golden light off the silver and touched sparks in the crystal wine goblets. Even though a pianist tickled keys, accompanying a bassist who stroked sensual notes from her instrument.

Even though she was with the only man who'd ever melted her frigid libido and still managed to kindle heat in her when he seemed completely oblivious to her presence.

He ordered starters and painful silence ensued.

"Bina got to the room all right?" Of course she had or he wouldn't have left Zephyr. *Try harder, Jaya.*

"She looks like you," he said with a lift of his brows. "It

was startling. Made me think that's what our—your daughter could look like, if you had one. People must make that mistake often?"

"All the time." She swallowed, trying not to latch onto what she thought he'd meant to say. *Our.*

More silence. This dress, coming out, it was a huge mistake. He wasn't comfortable so she couldn't relax.

Theo eyed Jaya's tense posture. His own prickling tension was at maximum. She couldn't relax, probably because she felt threatened by his mood.

A pile of ferocious curses piled up in the back of his throat. He was so angry, he could barely think straight. Damn it, why did this exquisite woman keep winding up beyond his reach?

He wished he could take back his confession of his desire. He'd come on strong, had taken a lot of heart from her saying she was still attracted to him, but the rest... Hell, no, nothing between them was simple anymore. What had seemed like an obvious solution, marriage, was now a minefield.

And yet...

Bloody hell, he had to let it go. Maybe if he hadn't told her *before* she explained about her past that he was still hot for her. Maybe if he wasn't currently simmering with insane want, but wow, *that dress.*

Ah, hell, it wasn't the dress. He'd seen a thousand scraps of silk and sequins on a thousand beautiful women and this wasn't the most elaborate or provocative. It was exactly Jaya's style: pretty and feminine, accented with fine metallic strands, but rather sweet overall.

It wasn't the dress that smelled so good he felt drugged. He didn't want to run his hands over sheer fabric and frilly ruffles. He didn't want to taste stitching.

Her skin called out to him. Her lips.

He forced himself to look away and sip his ice water.

Cool his head. Somehow he had to kill off this attraction so he wasn't scaring or intimidating her.

"I shouldn't have told you," she said so softly he wasn't sure he heard her. When he glanced at her, her delectable mouth was pouted in misery. "It changes how you see me, doesn't it?"

"Yes," he allowed with brutal honesty, distantly aware that wasn't the right thing to say, but he struggled with emotions at the best of times and these were some of the worst he'd ever encountered.

Her deep brown eyes widened in a flinch of stark pain, gaze not lifting from the tabletop. Then she struggled to regain her composure, brow working not to wrinkle, mouth trembling until she caught her bottom lip with her teeth.

"For God's sake, Jaya. I don't think *less* of you. I hate myself. I shouldn't have taken advantage of you the way I did. You deserved better." His voice came out low and jagged, as if he'd smoked ten packs of cigarettes and was hardly breathing through the thickness clogging his lungs.

"Better than the first real pleasure I've known with a man? Better than Zephyr?" she challenged shakily.

He was rarely shocked speechless. When he pinned his lips, it was because he was prudent, not because he couldn't think of what to say, but her words blanked his mind. Bali had been a mistake, he kept telling himself, but she seemed to be lifting his actions out of reprehensible into something that was almost exalted. He didn't know how to process that.

"It's like your back, Theo. I'll always have scars, but they fade a little more each year. If you make enough good memories, they push the bad ones away."

He sat back, startled by her insight. He snorted. "I guess that's my problem," he admitted as realization dawned. "I've never made any good memories. Well, maybe one." He couldn't help the significance in the cut of his glance toward her. She was so beguiling. Their night together eclipsed every other memory he had.

Even in the low candlelight, he could tell that her brown skin darkened. Her flustered hands moved into her lap and she ducked her head.

"You know I wouldn't—" he began, catching himself from reaching for her. She was such a panacea for him. He wanted to eat her up. Drown in her. She was everything good that could ever be for him, but he couldn't be greedy about it. He had to hang on to his control.

Her reserve was more than natural modesty, he reminded himself. Her sexual inhibitions were well founded and he'd take a thousand beltings before he'd frighten her with his desire. If she had used him that one night, because she was having a brave moment, well, lucky him.

"I'm glad if our night is a good memory for you, but I don't expect it to happen again. If that's why you're reluctant to marry me, we can keep it platonic." He couldn't believe those words had left his mouth, but having even a small part of her in his life seemed like better than nothing.

Again her eyes widened like she was enduring a wave of agony. "Because now you know I'm soiled goods and don't want—"

"What? No!" His hand went onto her arm involuntarily. He had to hiss in a breath as he strove for control and lifted his touch away, but only managed to transfer it to the back of her chair. Leaning in close, he said, "If you think I'm not aching to make more first-class memories with you, then you are even more naïve than I've always feared. The appeal you have for me... It scares *me*, Jaya. You'd be terrified if you knew how intense my desire is."

He forced himself to retreat into his own space. A deep gulp of ice water did nothing to clear his head. The glossy window reflected his iron hard expression back to him as

he braced himself for her to bolt. He should have kept all
that to himself.

She sat in quiet contemplation, then confessed softly, "I
don't know why you're the only man who makes me feel...
well, *anything,* but you are. *That* scares me. I feel like I
could be at your mercy, not because of your will. It would
be lack of my own."

Excitement pierced him, the arrow so thickly coated
in desire he had to close his eyes and concentrate on his
breathing. Swearing under his breath, he opened his eyes
and let her see the hunger in him, just for a second.

"You're killing me. You know that," he accused, voice
buried in a chest.

Her lashes flickered and she quivered like one of those
plucked strings that were trying to set a calm mood while
he was a werewolf fighting to stay inside his human skin.

"I don't mean to," she whispered. "I just want to be
honest."

A bleak laugh escaped him. "It would be a helluva better
foundation for a marriage than my parents had."

She cocked her head. "They lied to each other?"

"My mother did, yeah," he said, distaste curling his lip.
"She said Nic was my father's. When the truth came out,
things turned ugly. The only way any of us coped was to
pretend. We acted like we didn't remember Nic, like we
didn't hate our mother, like we weren't scared of our father."
He clenched his teeth, startled by the ugly truths that poured
like fresh blood from a new wound. "Your honesty isn't
comfortable for me. I'm not used to it, but... It's reassuring."

She offered a crooked smile.

His heart tipped on its edge, making him bold enough
to add, "So whatever you're thinking about how I might
be thinking of you differently, it's only that I'm trying to
offer you reassurance as well. I won't force you into anything, Jaya. Not marriage, not my bed."

Her watchful gaze wasn't easy to bear. He felt like his entire future hung in the balance.

"I believe you," she murmured, leaning on her elbows. "And I don't feel coerced. I know that marriage is probably best for Zephyr, but a lifetime is a long time, Theo. I can't just leap in. I need to know what it would look like first."

"I have no idea," he admitted, tensing against the million ways he could fail her without even being aware of it. "What do you want it to look like?"

She sat back to consider that and her gaze snagged on the couple at the next table as they rose and moved onto the dance floor. Her face became younger, cast with the yearning of a woman who loved to move to music.

"Would you dance with me?" she queried.

"Of course." He stood and held out his hand while calling himself a shameless ass for seizing the excuse to touch her. Maybe it was even a small test to see if she would accept his hands on her. He could live within just about any limit, so long as he knew what it was. He was going crazy not knowing where his lines were with her.

"I meant, you know, are you the kind of man who would dance with his wife?"

"You weren't asking? Then I am. Will you dance with me, Jaya?" He picked up her hand, oddly pleased with the shy smile she hid with a dip of her chin.

He'd learned early that the guy who was willing to dance got laid. He was proficient at most of the ballroom moves, but she made him hyperaware of himself as he fit them together, especially because he was on guard against being too aggressive. He wasn't quite as smooth as he'd wish, but he wasn't standing on her painted toes, either.

She was awkward, her hesitation seeming more from surprise and unfamiliarity with formal dancing than apprehension. After settling her hand on his shoulder and her fingers into his palm, she took a step forward instead of back, then cringed in horror.

He grinned. "It's fine, just follow my lead."

She did and because she was naturally graceful and rhythmic, they moved well together—not unlike the way they'd meshed in Bali. It was her same quiet trust that made it possible, heating him to his core as he absorbed it, solidifying his need to take great care with her, stoking his need.

"Question answered?" he managed to say, trying to keep things light.

"You're sneaky," she accused. "Maybe you don't bully or pressure, but you're not above seduction, are you?"

He stopped dancing and drew in a deep breath, harking back to when he'd done everything he could to lure her by her own desire into his bed. "Jaya—"

"It's okay, Theo. I don't know what I'm doing when it comes to men." She nudged him back into leading. "I've never danced like this, never been on a real date. If you don't make advances nothing will happen because I don't know how. That's really why I'm scared to say I'll marry you. You're the first man who's asked."

Reservations paralyzed him, but when he used the excuse of an approaching pair of dancers to pull her close, his misgivings slipped from his mind. The contact of her abdomen hitting his hips detonated a subdued explosion that drained his thoughts.

Her lips parted as they held the pose for an extended few seconds, eyes locked.

She took a sudden step back, but didn't release his hand when he relaxed his hold on hers. Chewing her lip, she seemed to debate whether to continue their dance.

"I'm always like this around you," he admitted under his breath, throwing his ego into the wind. It might be the dumbest thing in the world to think this would reassure her, but if they had agreed on nothing else, they were being honest with each other. Maybe, just maybe, if she knew she could trust him, he could have her in his bed again someday. "Every time I saw you in Bali, I was aroused. Just knowing I would see you would do this to me. I've only ever acted on it the once, Jaya, when you wanted me to."

They still weren't moving, only holding the half embrace while music and couples swirled around them. He searched for uneasiness in her, but her eyes were clouding with confusion and... Was it desire?

If he cupped her breast right now, he wondered, would he find her nipple pebbled and sensitive, aching for the pull of his mouth?

He swallowed, dying as he balanced on the knife's edge between hell and ecstasy.

"Would you kiss me, please?" she asked softly. "I've been wondering—"

He did, not debating, just grasping at permission to capture her parted lips with his. Deep in the back of his mind he reminded himself, *Easy. Go slow.*

It was agonizing to hold himself back. She was so exquisite, her mouth the pillowy satin welcome that tortured his dreams. By some feat of inhuman discipline, he kept his hand light when he clasped the side of her neck where she was warm and soft. He raked his mouth across hers in gentle ravishment, drinking in the clove and nutmeg taste of her.

Jaya liked these extra high heels. Her neck didn't hurt from tilting up to Theo's kiss. Her arms rose of their own accord to curl behind his neck. She opened to the tip of his tongue with a hitch of her breath and started to arch into him.

His hands hardened on her hips, pressing her into her shoes as he lifted his head.

"I was wondering, too." His voice sounded like it originated in the bottom of his chest and came out in a purr like a high performance engine. "We're still incredible together. Make sure you take that into consideration." He circled his thumbs on her hips.

She ducked her laugh into his collarbone, hand pressed to where his heart slammed in the tense cage of his ribs. *Oh, Theo.* She had missed him so much. In this second, all she could think was that she wanted to spend the rest of her life with him, feeling like this.

It reminded her of that fearful moment in Bali when she'd closed her eyes and grasped at her own future. There had been consequences to her actions that she hadn't fore-seen. She ought to show a little more sense this time. Mar-riage was the oldest form of subjugation in history.

But she didn't believe it would be that way with him. Perhaps she was fooling herself, but she felt more like a mammal with the mate she was meant for. Whether she said yes today or years from now, no man was ever going to have this same effect on her. In her heart she was al-ready tied to Theo. Hesitating to make it official seemed like fighting the inevitable.

On the other hand, was money and sex enough? Could Theo ever give her the things she really craved from a life-time with a man?

"Our food has arrived," he said, nudging her back to their table.

Her pulse jittered from his touch as she sat down and tried to take in the scorched scallops atop crunchy potato cakes.

When they were alone she asked, "Where would we live?"

"With me," he deadpanned. "That's the point."

She laughed, but he only scowled as he chewed and swallowed.

"I need to talk to Adara about curtailing the worst of my travel. Whether you marry me or not, I have to be available to Zephyr, but I'll always have to do some globe-trotting. I don't particularly care for Paris as a base, but it's closer to India than New York. Could you stand it?"

"Could you?" she challenged, taking in the tight grip he had on his fork with a tilt of her equilibrium into caution. "I'm actually quite flexible. I've started over in new places several times. You live in your helicopter. You're used to doing what you like. Having a wife and child would turn your life upside down, Theo."

"I'm aware," he stated flatly, setting down his utensils to stroke restless hands up and down his thighs. "And I won't claim that I'd be easy to live with, especially in the beginning, but I keep coming back to what I can offer you in terms of security and protection. Marriage is the simplest way to accomplish that."

She ought to be flattered, she supposed. There was a type of caring in his bland statement, even if it was the kind one usually showed to, say, an expensive boat or maybe a herd of cattle. On some level he valued her, she deduced. That was nice, but it wasn't enough to sustain a marriage.

Their conversation drifted to what kind of placement she could have with Makricosta's, as his wife or not, and they didn't talk about marriage again until they'd returned to the suite.

First they had to release the matronly Madame Begnoche and Theo had to negotiate a peace treaty with Bina. She was very sad to learn that Theo wanted Zephyr living with him rather than coming to South America with her and Quentin.

"Pyaari beti," Jaya reminded gently, "You know I was going to stay in France and not come with you and your papa."

"I know, but, but…" Her voice threatened to crack into sobs.

Theo extracted a business card and wrote on it before he

handed it to Bina. "This is my personal mobile. Call any-time you are missing Zephyr. We probably won't be able to come to you that day, but we'll try to visit within the week. Or, if your father agrees, I'll bring you to visit him. We'll work it out, I promise."

"Thank you," she said in a heavy but mollified voice, blinking her damp doe eyes.

When she held up her arms, Theo didn't get it. Jaya had to touch his shoulder and nod. "She wants to hug you."

"Oh, um." Clearing his throat, he went down on one knee so Bina could squeeze his neck with her spindly arms. He patted her back awkwardly and deflated with a heavy exhale after she left to meet Oscar and the limo, Theo's treat.

"Thank you," Jaya said to him. "But you can't keep of-fering to fly me and my family around the world."

"Why not?"

Because I haven't agreed to marry you, she almost said, but she suspected it didn't matter. He'd do it regardless. "You're a soft touch when it comes to kids, aren't you?"

"I don't know what that means, but having Nic disappear on us was a trauma I don't want to drop on my own son."

Oh, right. She swallowed, watching him run a fingertip along his eyebrow. She wondered if he was looking for an-other argument to persuade her to marry him.

"Theo." She sat heavily in the middle of the sofa.

His head came up, expression patient.

Her heart grew achy and she had to look at her finger-nails. "I don't want to string you along wondering what you have to do to convince me to marry you. I'm not hesitating because I'm afraid of going to bed with you."

She bit her lips, keeping her head down while stealing a quick peek upward, noting that she had his attention, one thousand percent. He was virility personified, all his masculine features sharpened, his wide shoulders tense and defined beneath his crisp white shirt.

"Actually, I am a little nervous about that. I've had a baby since the last time and it's not like I've had a lot of practice..." She swallowed.

"We'll be amazing, Jaya. Just like last time." His voice reverberated deep in his chest.

If she hadn't been sitting, she would have fallen, he made her so weak. She grasped for the words she needed to say. "I'm not afraid you'd be violent or disrespectful, either. I know I could trust you about most things."

"But not all things." Tone cracked with a jag of disbelief, he recoiled in hurt.

She swallowed, knowing this would be difficult.

"You didn't call me back," she said in a small voice. "I know you said you wouldn't, but..." She tried to shrug off how foolish she felt, how bare this fantasy of hers left her. "I thought I was different. I thought you liked me."

His face transformed in slow degrees, falling from intense focus on her to inward comprehension, into lost hope and finally, self-hatred.

"I don't expect you to love me," she rushed to say, even though it tore open something inside her. "But I always wanted to marry for love." Such a girlish dream, so romantic and silly. That's the message she'd always received, but she still wanted it. "I need something between us that's not just practicality and hormones. Those things aren't a real bond. They're not something you fight for. But if you had any feelings for me at all..."

He did his thing where he froze. Not shrinking. He didn't cringe, but he braced himself. Like he refused to show how vulnerable he felt, while at the same time expected great pain. "I don't understand why you'd want me to."

Careful, she urged herself. He wasn't being arrogant or callous. He probably, genuinely didn't understand. She heard the barest inflection on *me* in his statement and knew this was more about his low opinion of himself than lack of regard for her.

Licking her lips, choosing her words with care, she said, "Everyone wants to be liked. Don't you?"

He shook his head. "It doesn't matter to me either way." Because he'd been reviled by someone who was supposed to love him. The abraded edges of her heart frayed and stung.

"What about your sister? Surely it matters to you that she loves you?"

His shoulder jerked, almost like he was deflecting a blow. "I'm sure she values my loyalty. I take satisfaction in knowing she can count on me."

He only took what pride he gave himself, would never ask for a smidgen more even from a woman he'd take a bullet to protect. How utterly abandoned he must have felt to mold himself into someone so inaccessible.

"Well, I want to be liked," Jaya said with one hand cupped in the palm of the other, trying to project calm control when emotion tore at her throat. "I'd like whatever attraction you feel toward me to be for more than whatever parts of me fit into lingerie. Because I think you're a very good-looking man, but when I say I'm attracted to you, I mean that I *like* you, Theo." *Love,* a voice inside her contradicted, but it was such a huge admission to be in love that she pressed it back into her subconscious, not quite ready to be that vulnerable.

Still, as she lifted her gaze, she was absolutely defenseless, like he must be able to read that her feelings were so much stronger than she was admitting, but she didn't want to scare him, only let him see she was sincere.

"Jesus, Jaya," he whispered in a ragged breath, looking away.

His image swam before her brimming eyes, but she

thought she'd seen a flinch of great anguish, like her words had touched a very raw part of him. He rubbed his hand across his jaw.

"For God's sake, why?" he expelled with disbelief.

Oh, you poor, poor man. She rose and went to him, unable to sit so far from him when he was hurting so much. Cupping his head, she forced his tortured expression to face hers.

"Why do I like you? You're a good man, Theo. When I told you about my assault, you didn't ask what I was wearing or whether I did something to encourage it. You never once lost patience with those babies even though they kept us up half the night. You protected your little brother when you were barely old enough to—"

"Shh, don't." He pulled her into his chest, crushing her so tight she could barely draw breath. His heart pounded against her breast and she felt his swallow where his damp throat was pressed to her temple. His breaths moved harshly in his nostrils as he tried to regain control, holding her against the rise and fall of his shaken breaths.

She let herself soften into him, hoping her signal of acceptance would penetrate.

His own arms loosened a fraction and she wound her arms around his chest. Their embrace became mutual. Tight and close, man and woman. He cupped the back of her head and rubbed his chin on her hair.

"People hate to see me coming," he said after a long time. "I criticize how they're doing things, ask for paperwork they can't find, make them account for items they think are insignificant. You always smiled at me, no matter what I asked for. I was never an imposition to you. That's so rare for me."

He combed his fingers through her hair while she closed her eyes against a sharp sting, feeling dampness gather on her lashes and keeping them hidden in his shirt, certain he'd stop holding her if he knew how moved she was.

"Do I *like* you?" he continued. "I don't have friends. I don't know how that works. I wish I could say I loved you, that I could give you everything you want from a man. Knowing you want love tells me I don't deserve you."

She hitched in a breath of protest, but he was continuing, arms tightening a fraction to keep her in place.

"But I'm not selfless enough to give you up. I want you in my life. Not just because my mouth waters when I think of you naked. Hell, you can feel how I'm reacting now, but there are a lot of beautiful women out there. There's only one you. You *are* special, Jaya."

She hugged him hard, biting her lips because they were quivering. "Thank you for saying that."

"But it's not enough, is it?" He slid heavy hands to her shoulders and eased her back a step. "You do deserve better."

Here was the crossroads again. She couldn't know if marrying him was the right choice unless she made it and looked back on having lived with it, but she couldn't hurt him by rejecting him. All she could do was remember how perfect they had been once and believe that, with time, they could surpass it.

Without breathing, courage gathered into a tight knot in her middle, she picked up his hand to cradle it against her cheek. "You're going to have to trust me when I say that I would be honored and privileged to be your wife," she quavered.

He searched her gaze, a small frown pulling his brows. "Are you saying—"

She nodded, unable to help smiling when he was so plainly taken by surprise. "I would like to marry you, Theo."

The flash of male triumph that streaked into his fierce

visage might have frightened her if there wasn't a helping of relief beneath it, endearingly softening his ruthless expression. In the next instant, he shuttered himself so thoroughly, she wondered if she had seen any reaction at all.

"Thank you. We'll get a ring in the morning."

And the CFO was back, armed with his tasks. Nevertheless, she'd seen behind the curtain and knew there was something there, even if it wasn't very clearly defined.

"I don't need a ring," she dismissed, and reluctantly let her hands drop. She didn't know how to bring herself out from intense emotional intimacy to distance with the swiftness that he did. A chill made her cross her arms and self-protect.

"I want to do this properly," he insisted, then grimaced. "I suppose that means we should wait until our wedding night. How long does it take to plan a wedding?"

"Wait for what? Oh." She ducked her head to hide that she was blushing, partly because she was dense enough not to have got his meaning right away, but also because she was disappointed. "We don't have to," she murmured.

"I want you to be sure." He pushed his hands into his pockets, but she could see he was still aroused. He was trying not to touch her, she realized, and glittering delight bounced through her at her effect on him.

"I am sure." She lifted her face so he could see she wasn't teasing, but she didn't know how to flirt or invite. Arousal was still too new.

"Sure about all of it," he clarified with a rueful look. "Given our track record, I'd knock you up by midnight. As you said, this is your first proposal. I won't trap you."

A small smile touch her lips at the prospect of him forcing a shotgun wedding, but another thought occurred and it was a big one. "Do you want more children?"

His expression blanked in surprise. "I haven't given it any thought. Hell, last week I didn't want any. Today…I don't know. Being a single child sounds lonely for Zephyr, doesn't it? I mean, Demitri is a complete pain in the ass, but I can't imagine not having him around."

"It's open for discussion, then?" she confirmed. This was a deal-breaker for her.

"Yes," he said firmly. "But let's give ourselves a chance to get to know one another again first." His gaze feathered over her cheek and lit on her mouth.

He knew how to say things that both flattered and intrigued. Despite his sweetly suggestive remark, however, a very somber mood came over him.

Her smile faded. "What's wrong?"

"Not one thing." He cupped her face and kissed her with startling tenderness. "You're very lovely, Jaya. How long until I can call you my wife?"

"I don't know." Her heart turned over and already she wondered if she'd done the right thing. "A few months?"

He grimaced.

"Unless you want a small wedding," she rushed to say. "That could be arranged in a week or two."

"I want to do this right." His hands fell to her shoulders and he looked over her head, his expression weighted by heavy thoughts. His hands massaged, but distractedly. Like he'd slipped miles away from her. "You'll want your family to come."

"My parents, yes, but it doesn't have to be a big deal. I've never dreamed of being the center of a society wedding. I can't imagine you have, either." She nudged his stomach playfully.

"More like suffered nightmares." His mouth twisted with aversion. "But we have business associates in New York and relatives in Greece who should be invited."

"Big weddings are expensive."

"Do *not* worry about the cost." He stepped away to state

decisively, "We should be able to make a strong statement in six weeks."

"A statement?" she repeated.

"As opposed to a splash."

"Okay." She tried to read his inscrutable expression.

"You should get some sleep. I'll listen for Zephyr," he said.

"You're staying up to work?" The way he shut her out was not the way she thought an engagement should start.

"I need to think. I'm used to having more time with my own thoughts than I've had in the last few days."

"Oh. Of course." She tried not to take that as a slight. *She* hadn't initiated this chain of events. If only he'd kiss her again, so the fragile bond between them would grow another layer, rather than fade. But he didn't.

"Good night," she said, confidence dwindling as she went to her room.

CHAPTER ELEVEN

As someone whose life had changed overnight before, Jaya had learned to prefer a gradual, thoughtful approach to making shifts in her world. After her abrupt departure from India, she'd had months of notice before her move to Bali. Once settled, she'd dug in, comfortable in her role there. France had been a culture shock, but she'd had family to cushion the blow.

Nothing could have prepared her, probably not even time, for being pulled into the Makricostas' world. First she'd had to quit her job, which had been a tough decision even though Adara emailed with three job offers "to consider when the time is right." Then there was the travel, flitting up to London for two nights because Theo had a meeting and a thing.

"What kind of thing?" she'd asked when he'd requested she accompany him.

"A presentation. We paid to refurbish a historical building. One of the royals will be there so I've been elected to represent."

One of the royals. Like this was normal.

Which meant an upgrade to her wardrobe. No longer did she own a few nice outfits. Every time she turned around, Theo was bringing in a designer or a stylist or squiring her into a shop where the *prêt-à-porters* didn't even have price tags.

"I thought women enjoyed shopping," he said at one point.

"But the cost! I'm not even working."

He quirked a brow at her. "Do you have any idea how much money I make? How well I invest it? I never spend any."

Except on his fleet of airplanes and helicopters. He did some flitting of his own in those, disappearing to South America and Japan for a couple of days without her. She couldn't complain. She put off her separation from Bina as long as she could and needed the time to pack up her life, plan a wedding and look for a suitable home in New York.

The city was incredible. They spent a week there and she looked forward to living there permanently. However, the bit where Theo ensconced her in the family suite at the Makricosta Grand and visited his apartment without her bothered her immensely. It was too small for them, even in the interim, she agreed. She also understood he was a private man who liked his own space. Plus, as he pointed out oh-so-reasonably, here at the hotel she had help on tap—boy, did she have help. She used to be the one who jumped when a Makricosta rang. It was bizarre to be on the receiving end of that level of service from people a lot further up the corporate food chain than she'd ever been.

Then, just when her insecurities began to get the best of her and she convinced herself he'd be the most hands-off, distant husband, that this whole thing was a terrible mistake, he reassured her. After practically ignoring her all day in front of the real estate agent, he drew her into his arms as they closed the door of the hotel suite and kissed her breathless, saying when they came up for air, "I've been wanting to do that all day. You look amazing." She happened to be wearing one of her own modest navy skirts with a canary lace top over a lemon-colored cami. Nothing flashy or fantastic.

Then, when they'd decided on a penthouse apartment
a few blocks from Adara and Gideon's, with a view of
the park and a rooftop patio and pool, she'd watched him
close the deal with an emotionless handshake. When the
agent left them alone, an ominous silence descended, worrying her.

She rocked Zephyr on her hip. "Are you sure? You don't
look pleased."

"You said you loved it." He snapped his head around.

"I do! You're the one who went into lockdown when
I said I thought this was the one and could we have one
more look."

He didn't like it when she called him on his standoff-
ishness. She was learning his tells and noted the tick in his
brow and the muscle that clenched in his jaw. But being
blunt was the only way to get him to open up enough for
her to understand him and not feel closed out.

"I didn't mean to." He kept one hand fisted in his pocket,
his mouth tense and outlined in white.

The look he flashed at her was both impatient with himself and…not distrustful, but like he wasn't sure of her.
With a cross noise, he shrugged. He kept a proud bearing,
but it was like he was headed to the gallows, he was so
stiff and withdrawn as he pulled his hand from his pocket.

"You know I'm the furthest thing from a romantic," he
said gruffly. "But I thought if we decided this would be
home, it would be a good time to give you this, as a sort
of… Hell, I don't know." He showed her the sparkle he held.
"An official start?"

She gasped. "You picked up the ring?" They'd chosen
the stones two weeks ago, but she hadn't expected to see
the finished setting until right before the wedding.

"I figured if you said yes to the apartment, you were
probably going through with the wedding so…"

He was nervous!

Too awed to laugh, she rushed forward to kiss him. Zephyr got in the way, of course, little fists grabbing at Theo and catching a chest hair so he winced and pulled away long enough to take him. Then he pulled her back into him like a pirate grabbing a wench, angling her over his arm as he kissed her like he really meant it. Like he wanted to devour her because he desired her so much.

Jaya straightened her ring on her finger now, the memory of their kiss embedded into the piece as irrevocably as the oval cut sapphire. The goldsmith had created a setting that looked as if he'd cut a blond band open then twisted it, setting the rare purple stone between the scrolled ends. He'd finished the tails with ever shrinking pink diamonds. The result a piece with such femininity, it made the extravagance subtle and elegant.

Much like the stunning mini-villa behind her, she thought ruefully, lifting her gaze to the view of the Parthenon lit yellow-gold by the fading sun. They'd decided on Athens for the wedding. It was a less grueling flight for her family and worked for his.

It was like a fairy tale, but she'd had another run of doubts as recently as last night. They'd had dinner with Adara and Gideon. Nic and Rowan had their own apartment in the city, but had joined them in the family suite. The babies had reunited into a loud, happy flock that Theo had stood apart from while the others dove in with quick hands to retrieve a dropped toy or change a bottom. Gideon, as Adara had predicted, took to Zephyr like he'd made him, rolling on the floor with all the children, far more relaxed than she'd ever expected the cool, stern Director of the Board for the Makricosta empire to be.

Theo, on the other hand, wasn't as forward with his affection, waiting for the little ones to come to him, saying something about them probably not remembering him.

After a night of agonizing whether he shared her dream

for a loving family, she'd woken to find Theo on his back on the lounge floor, Zephyr lifted like a superhero above him, both of them laughing as Theo lowered him to make growling noises against his little belly. It was exactly the game Gideon had played with all the children the night before.

She'd pretended she needed her phone to hide her moved tears.

He just needs someone to show him how to love, she reasoned. She was that person. Somehow she'd overcome her mistrust and was falling for him. It was only fair to believe he had the capacity to love her back, given time and enough trust between them.

A door opened and closed in the suite behind her.

Her ruminations fell away and she smiled with anticipation, expecting him to come to her. Sometimes he checked on Zephyr first, if he was napping, which he was. Then they'd neck until they were breathless and oh, why weren't they married yet? She was growing impatient to feel his skin, his hands, *him*.

Swallowing the rush of feeling, she blinked the smeared colors of the Parthenon from her eyes and turned with a beaming smile.

And saw Theo making out with a woman against the wall, just inside the entry doors of the penthouse.

No.

Squinching the wetness from her eyes, she swiped her forearm over them as she stumbled on bare feet across the marble tiles of the rooftop garden, around the end of the pool and up to the point where the air-conditioning of the interior blended with the heat of the outdoors.

Maybe that was her own body causing the hot and cold baffling through her as she stared with disbelief at a familiar back. His shoulders flexed beneath his white shirt as he guided a woman's leg to his hip then slid his hand under the edge of her polka dot skirt. Sharp pink talons poked through his brown hair as they kissed.

A million thoughts whirled like tornado debris in her mind. He had said he was going for a haircut. That wasn't the shirt he was wearing this morning. Where did he think she was that he would bring some floozy back to where they were staying?

Nothing in the world could have prepared her for this. Except a senior chambermaid had taught her what to do in exactly this situation on her first day of work ten years ago.

"Housekeeping!" Jaya blurted in a shrill voice.

With a squeal, the woman's platform sandal clapped to the floor.

He barely lifted his head. "Come back another time." He chased another kiss.

It was Theo's voice, but the way he ignored her wasn't Theo.

"Demitri?" she hazarded.

His head came up again and he sent a laconic glance over his shoulder. "Jaya?"

"You're married?" the woman gasped.

"Hell, no. My brother's fiancée. Jaya, we're going to need some privacy. Can you…?" He gave her a "shove-off" motion.

"Of course." She grasped for her wits and searched for her purse. "I've been waiting for the baby to wake so I could go shopping, but if you'll listen for him—"

Demitri released his partner and reached for the door-knob, blocking Jaya's exit as he pressed his mate through it. "Wait for me at the elevator," he told her as he kissed her pout and gave her a pat on the behind before closing her out.

Jaya returned her purse to the side table and folded her arms, waiting for his next move with her brows in her hair-line.

He turned to her with an amused smile. "Well played."

Now she saw him properly, she could see the resemblance was strong, but not identical. He was obviously younger and not quite as handsome as Theo. *Too* devilish.

"I thought leaving babies with bachelor uncles was how your family does things."

He snorted. "I remembered you as shy and quiet. Made me wonder where Theo found the…"

His pause prompted her to fill in one of the thousand slang words men used to describe the source of their fertility and courage. She held her breath, waiting to hear which vulgar term he would pick.

"…temerity," he provided with a wicked tilt of his grin, "to date you."

He was a brat, through and through. She'd known it from her few interactions with him and now that Theo had explained about their family she even understood why. Demitri got away with his cheeky, outrageous behavior because no one stopped him.

"Speaking of dates, is that yours for the wedding? Because your family is staying in another suite. I'm expecting mine here shortly."

He shrugged off the information. "No, I don't even know her name. I picked her up in the bar." He was utterly without shame or consideration for others.

Genuinely curious about that, she cocked her head. "Why do you like to take people so off guard? Does it give you a sense of power to introduce chaos?"

He barely blinked, but narrowed his eyes in reassessment. "Here I thought I was behaving. The last time Theo was engaged, I picked up his bride."

When she caught a shocked breath, he smiled.

"He never mentioned that?"

She could have kicked him in his temerities, she was so infuriated by his smug air at having disarmed her. How could he do something so awful as seduce his brother's intended? And be proud of it?

Why hadn't Theo told her?

"He knows you're not my type," was the best retort she could manage.

The door lock hummed then opened.

Theo paused to take in Demitri slouched beside the door and Jaya standing across the other side of the lounge, arms crossed in dismay.

"Jaya was just reminding me I'm not her type," Demitri said flippantly. "Good thing I've been preapproved down the hall."

Theo stopped Demitri's exit with two straight fingers poked into his chest.

Jaya found herself holding her breath, never having seen him angry, not like that. Instant and icy cold, completely ready to be aggressive and deadly. His mood was doubly volatile because he didn't lash out, only asked with deadly flatness, "Did he make a move on you?" He didn't take his eyes off his brother.

"N-no," she managed, arms aching where she had them wrapped around herself.

"Don't," Theo said to Demitri. "Ever. I have my limits. You've just found one."

Jaya's insides trembled, all of her shaken by Theo's possessive, protective words. She wanted to be reassured it proved he cared for her, but she was still reeling from the news that he'd been engaged once before and hadn't told her. Had he loved that other woman? Was that the real reason he couldn't love her?

The thought was as bad as those poisoned few seconds when she'd thought it was him in the clinch against the wall.

Demitri calmly moved Theo's hand aside, like he was opening a gate. He walked out without a word.

Theo watched him for a split second, the muscle in his

jaw pulsing, before he stepped in and closed the door. "I'll assume it was garden variety obnoxiousness on his part that has you looking so peeved?"

"Actually it was learning you were engaged before. Were you going to tell me?"

CHAPTER TWELVE

THEO SAW THE hurt Jaya made no effort to disguise and suppressed a flinch of guilt. At the same time, his heart pounded like a pile driver. He and Demitri had their moments, but he'd never been as close to getting physical with his little brother as a few seconds ago. Violence was wrong, but if Demitri had touched Jaya, had scared her...

Such a rush of complex emotions strangled him, his instinct was to turn around and walk out, find somewhere private to pull himself together and come back when he felt in control again.

Maybe if Jaya had been angry and accusing he could have walked away from her. Instead she had that vulnerable look about her, the one that wrenched his heart. Like she was exposing her throat and it was up to him to prove he wouldn't rip it out.

"Zeph sleeping?" he asked.

"He went down twenty minutes ago."

His wingman wouldn't provide a distraction then.

He rubbed his face, trying to push his expression back into stoic when he was still unsettled by what he'd walked into. Amazing how he'd become addicted to entering cheerful disarray where a woman and baby greeted him with smiles, maybe some homey smells, and he had to pick a path across scattered toys, but always found a reward of physical affection at the end.

"Theo?" she prompted.

He squeezed the back of his neck. This was why he'd kept to superficial relationships for so long. One-night lovers asked surface questions with easy answers.

Still, the more time he spent with Jaya and Zeph, the more he craved. He liked hearing her sing in Punjabi to their son, liked the homemade food she cooked, liked the way she drew attention when they were out, pulling it off him as people took in her exotic beauty. She'd always been pretty, but with the professional styling taking her appearance up a notch, he had himself a knockout of a fiancée and couldn't wait to have her legally tied to him as his wife.

He was surprisingly impatient to lock in that life and now realized what had subconsciously been driving him.

But to admit it all to her? *Hell.*

"It's humiliating," he said, tossing his key card on a side table and moving into the suite a few steps, then halting in frustration. He could feel her rebuff from here. An invisible wall sat between them, dense as lead and heavy enough to compress his chest.

"When?" she asked in a strained voice. "Since Bali? Because I never heard anything about you getting married while I was working there. I'm sure I would have."

"It was years before that," he dismissed

That detail seemed to relieve a fraction of her distress, but she still stared at him, willing him to provide more details.

"My father arranged it," he forced himself to say.

"Arranged. But you were so disparaging when you thought I was quitting to go to France for an arranged marriage."

"That's why." Everything in him ached for distance and privacy, but a different, unfamiliar compulsion kept him frozen here, longing to close the gap between them. He was learning the only way was to pick his path through the minefield of his past. He hated it, but for her, he did it.

"Did you love her?" The tentative edge in her voice told him how hard that was for her to ask.

"No," he assured with a disgusted exhale. "She was a socialite, a party girl, the daughter of a well-respected New York businessman who was down on his luck. They wanted the connection to our family, my father wanted an heir…"

"You said you never wanted to be a father!"

"I didn't," he said, recalling such heavy dread it had stuck with him until he'd learned how it really was to have his own child. "But I didn't have a choice."

"Men always have a choice," she said with resentment. "They're never as helpless as women in these situations. She was probably under more pressure to go through with it than you were."

"No, I don't believe that." He never went back over those memories, they made him feel too pathetic, but she forced him to with her accusation. "You're right that I could have walked away from my inheritance," he allowed, "but I couldn't do that to Adara. Not after what happened to us once Nic was gone."

No one would ever know how close he'd come despite that. He'd forgotten how his sister had been the tipping point for him. He'd been scared for her. If he hadn't been there to protect her, no one would have been. His unhappiness with a marriage to a woman he didn't care about had seemed like nothing against Adara's safety.

Somehow, remembering his motive loosed the old shame off him. Yes, he'd been browbeaten and yes, it had been his choice to allow it. But he'd had a good reason.

"Demitri said he slept with her," Jaya said.

"He did." He felt nothing making that admission because the act had become the mortar he used to thicken and heighten the walls he used to protect himself. From then on, he'd held everyone even more firmly at a distance, even his siblings. Why in hell would anyone want to be close to him? He was second best to his outgoing, funny younger brother. Everyone preferred Demitri, given the choice.

Except Jaya. Maybe the seeds of his deep admiration had been born in seeing her deflection of men who came onto her, especially the ones who took for granted they could impress with a grin and a flash of money. She had smiles for everyone, but she reserved her warmest for grandfathers with arthritis or little boys who got off the elevator on the wrong floor.

"Why would he do that? Just to prove he could or…?" She shook her head in bafflement. "To hurt you?"

He drew in a breath that burned. "It wasn't just once for bragging rights. They had an affair. I don't know who started it and God knows I won't make excuses for him, but he was nineteen to her twenty-three. She happily drove to Manhattan and paraded herself through the lobby so all our staff could see them carrying on."

And his father had berated him, like it was his fault when he'd been half a state away finishing exams. *Such* impossible expectations. He swore if Zephyr never aspired to anything more ambitious than flipping burgers in a fast food shack, he'd make sure the boy knew he was proud of him.

"What did she say when you broke it off?"

Here came the degradation, but it was losing its potency as they talked of this. For too many years, he'd let this make him feel weak. He been strong. Enduring. "I didn't."

"Didn't break it off? But…Why not?"

The easy answer was, "I didn't have to. Adara convinced our father the publicity was too damaging to go through with it. By then Gideon was on the scene. Her engagement let me off the hook."

"You would have gone through with it?" She sounded appalled.

He was equally galled with himself, which is why he never revisited this ugly time, but he'd been a different man then. One who merely survived, not one who cared about thriving or his own happiness or anyone else beyond the one person who had always been there for him. Looking back, he barely recognized himself.

The turning point had been Bali, he saw now, and not because of Adara's call—even though that had been a catalyst. No, he'd begun thawing toward his siblings after that, but he couldn't have managed it if he hadn't had that night with Jaya. She'd begun the melt in him with her kind acceptance of his weakness that night. He only recognized now that it was her influence because he'd changed so much since he'd seen her again.

Shaking himself out of the stunning realization, he tried to answer.

"All of my options were terrible. If I'd broken it off, my father would have done anything to hurt me, including going after my mother and Adara." He'd make a different choice today. He was stronger. Because he had someone else in his corner.

Didn't he? She was still struggling to understand why he'd kept this from her.

"But not Demitri," she said. "I can see why you're so loyal to Adara. She's always had your back, but I don't know how you tolerate your brother. Or is that your normal interaction with him? Are you two always hostile?" She nodded toward the door.

"No, we get along. The past is water under the bridge." He forced himself to open hands that had clenched into fists as he recalled his anger when he'd come in to find Demitri with Jaya, her expression cross and distressed. "I wanted him to know there will never be any forgiveness where you're concerned." He leveled a stern glance at her.

"You'll tell me if he crosses any lines. I'm serious about this being a red one."

"Because he did it once before." She looked to her linked fingers.

"Because you have entrusted me to keep you safe. I'd die before I'd let you feel threatened by him or anyone." He'd take on anyone for her, he realized. Not because he approved of violence, but because she was that precious to him.

"Theo." Her head came up in alarm. "Don't talk about dying."

"Hey," he deflected with a snort. "I hope it doesn't come to anything drastic like that, but I bring so little to this relationship, Jaya." The tiny flame in him that he barely acknowledged would never be enough for her. "At least let me give you this much."

"That's not true." Tension distended her neck as she took his remark like a knife to the throat. Could she blame him for not bringing his heart to their marriage though, when his own had been so chronically kicked around? "You bring yourself. Stop thinking that's not enough."

The silence was so profound she couldn't look up. Then, even from across the room, she heard his swallow.

"Is it?" he asked in a ragged voice. "Because you brought Zeph and he's pretty damned incredible."

"He is, isn't he?" she said shamelessly. "But he's half yours so—" She took a few faltering steps toward him, then hesitated, not sure if he was ready to close the distance. The things he'd shared had been hard for him. She'd had to pull the details like teeth and there wasn't any anesthetic for things like this.

He met her halfway, his strong hands reaching out to take hers in a gentle grip. Her own clenched convulsively, grasping for something more than his steady strength, even though she knew she should be satisfied with that. It should be enough.

Pressing her trembling lips into a line, she searched his face.

He didn't like it and looked away, obviously not comfortable with her need for reassurance. She dipped her head, suffering another wave of doubt that he'd ever open his heart to her.

"I'm sorry," he said gruffly. "I should have told you myself, not left it so you'd find out like that. It was like what happened last night, when Gideon told Androu not to touch the light socket and that just made him more aware of them. I didn't want to put the idea into your head."

"That I could have an affair with Demitri? He floated that balloon years ago and I stabbed it with a pen."

Theo snorted, thumbs stroking over her knuckles. "I don't know why he has to behave like such an ass."

"You and Adara hold your lives under tight control. If he turns things upside down he gains the upper hand."

"Now how did you see that and I never have?" He leaned back to absorb that.

"You've spent so many years putting up shields, you can't always see past them."

He blinked in surprise, seeming disconcerted. "But you can."

"Sometimes," she said warily. "Does that bother you?"

He drew a deep breath. "It's not comfortable." His hands tightened on hers and he looked into her eyes, even though he winced as he did it, like it was a kind of torture to let her see inside him. "But…" He swallowed, then, "I trust you, Jaya. I know you're not going to use anything I tell you to hurt me."

His grip crushed her hands, but she didn't think he was aware of it. She squeezed back, feeling they stood on a precipice that, if they took this leap of faith, they could land in new, rich, broad territory.

"I would never want to hurt you. Not ever," she promised, then held her breath.

Bringing her hand to his mouth, he ran the knuckle of her ring finger along his lips. His breath clouded warmly against her skin as he spoke, making her wrist tingle.

"I think half the reason I still speak to Demitri after what he did is gratitude. Ultimately he got me out of a situation I didn't want."

"Really?" This didn't seem the deep confidence she half expected. "Do you think he did it on purpose?" she asked, wondering if that was digging too deep.

"Hell, no. He'd never show that kind of forethought, but he created the excuse and I was glad. Swear to me you'll never reveal that to him."

A giggle escaped her, part relief, part joy that he was confiding in her a little. "Cross my heart and hope to die."

He took a deep breath and looked down on her with something like pride and...affection? His expression had softened into amusement and tenderness. It almost looked like happiness and made her warm all the way to the soles of her feet. He was solemn as he cradled her face and caressed her cheek with the pad of his thumb.

"I can't wait to marry you."

"Really?" She wanted to smile, but she was dissolving under his look and couldn't seem to hold any part of herself steady. "Because I thought it was you at first, when Demitri came in. He made out with that woman right there in front of me and I thought for a horrible second it was you and we were finished. I was devastated," she admitted.

His mellow smile faded. "I'll kill him."

Her turn to set a hand against his smooth cheek, freshly shaved and smelling of something tangy and fresh. "But then I realized it couldn't be you because you'd never do that to me. I never expected I'd be able to trust a man this much, Theo. I wish I could tell you what a gift you've given me with that." She slid her other hand up his chest and around his neck so her breasts pressed into the hardness of his chest and her damp lips touched his ultra-smooth jaw.

He gathered her in, crushing her close in tight arms and releasing a shuddering breath against her ear.

They sought each other's mouths, colliding with practiced alignment, parted lips meeting and sealing, plunging her into a dark jungle of sultry heat and velvet sensations. Combing her fingers up the back of his head, she reveled in the short, freshly cut strands, the new haircut, exactly as he'd promised. The thought made her want to smile but he was kissing her too intently.

He rasped his tongue down her neck, one hand palming her breast, making intense sensations race into her loins. She clenched to contain the deliciousness there.

This was moving fast and a distant part of her wondered if she should be worried about that, but desire flowed through her veins in rivers of lava, making her burn for him.

"God, Jaya," he groaned, stilling her rocking hips against the hard ridge of his erection. "The next two days are going to kill me."

"Oh, Theo, I don't want to wait anymo—*oh!*"

He scooped her up, his strength like a conqueror's as he bounced her into a high clasp against his chest, his arousal evident in the flush on his cheekbones and the sheen on his feral half grin. "If you're not going to stop me, then I won't."

She slid her hand from his shoulder to his ear, pulling herself close enough to kiss where his pulse pounded like a hammer in his throat.

As he started down the hall, two sounds halted him: Zephyr's cry and a knock on the penthouse door.

He swore and she softly wailed, "Nooooo," as he let her feet slide to the floor.

"That's your family, isn't it?" His gruff voice was rueful. "Better now than in five minutes when we would have been naked. I'll get Zeph. I need to pull myself together."

Snickering, she kissed his chin and started to walk away. He yanked her back for another deep swift kiss that included a taste of France. Dazzled, she bounced off the wall on her way to greet her guests.

Despite his sexual frustration, which was more acute than he'd ever thought he could bear, Theo was riding a natural high. Jaya still wanted to marry him.

He hadn't consciously been aware of that niggling concern. She always responded so sweetly to him and even though they had their differences, they always seemed to work through them. Still, a voice inside him had kept harping that he wasn't enough.

She thought he was a gift, though, because she could trust him. He swelled with pride knowing how hard-won that kind of reliance was for her. The determination to protect her ran through him on a current of reverence and resolve. In a few days he would pledge to uphold her faith in him and he'd do it with every fiber of his being.

Speaking of gifts…

Lifting his freshly diapered son to eye level, he took a moment to absorb the awe of fatherhood. While the magnitude of responsibility still scared him, and he wasn't yet a hundred percent confident he'd be everything Zephyr needed, he was learning. For most of his life, he'd been driven by the need to be perfect so he wouldn't catch hell. Now, he yearned to do well so he could be a better father than he'd had.

"That sets the bar pretty low, doesn't it?" he murmured

to his son before he kissed the boy's forehead and carried him out to the main lounge.

Heated voices speaking Punjabi fell into a wall of blistering silence when he appeared. He'd picked up a few words from Jaya and was working on a speech for the wedding, but he wasn't good enough with the language to follow any of what had been said even if he'd properly heard it.

He was the last man to judge a family for dysfunction, but Jaya had seemed to be making progress with them. Her tone had been growing lighter of heart when she'd spoken of them while travel and wedding plans had fallen into place. He had been counting on her finding some emotional fulfillment through her relationship with her mother and sister to compensate for his own lack. It was important to him that he not cheat her of love, that he give her every chance for it since he couldn't provide it himself.

This wasn't love, though. This was a tight army of angry young men backing up a grizzled bear with a thick gray beard. Two older women sat on the sofa, one in green, the other in blue. They bookended a young woman in yellow and a dazed older man. Their clothing seemed extracolorful against the white leather of the furnishings, their expressions taxed. The women seemed to be trying to make themselves smaller while the young men puffed up their chests under crossed arms.

Jaya stood apart from all of them, her anxiety palpable. The way she dropped her gaze after an initial tense glance at him seemed almost apologetic.

Theo mentally swore. He might have been swimming naked through these sorts of shark-infested undercurrents all his life, but he'd never grown comfortable in them.

"Welcome," he managed in Punjabi, then zeroed in on the woman beside the frail, confused looking man who must be Jaya's father.

"Jaya has been eager to see you all." He hoped that

wasn't overstepping. He hated it when people tried to talk
for him. Forcing himself to move forward even though his
joints felt rusted, he added, "This young man has been waiting to meet his *Naniji,* which is…Gurditta?"

He guessed correctly at the woman in the green sari.

Jaya's mother gasped and stopped dabbing a tissue into
her eye, dropping it away so she could pull Zephyr into her
lap. Her tears turned to joy as she gathered up the wiggling
boy like a bundle of laundry that wanted to drop socks.

Whatever dark cloud had been hovering broke into
beams of sunlight for a second as Jaya drank in the sight
of her mother holding her son. Then she glanced at the
bearded man with a mix of defiance, resentment and—
Theo's heart took it like a stiletto—a remnant of shame.

Before he realized what he was doing, he had moved to
her side and set a firm arm across her back. Belatedly, he
wondered if his hand on her hip might be a familiarity that
would repel someone with traditional views, but he needed
her to know she wasn't alone. They needed to know if they
insulted her, they insulted him, and he was not a naïve girl
working in a call center.

"Thank you for coming," he said, falling back on manners because it was one of his few fail-safe strategies in
a passive-aggressive confrontation like this. "I imagine
you're tired from the flight. My sister has planned a reception for the families to meet this evening, but you have
a few hours to rest."

Jaya's uncle, because that's who the hard-ass old grouch
had to be, said something in Punjabi.

Theo looked to her. She had said they all spoke at least
a little English and that her father would be the toughest
to communicate with because of his injury.

With a level stare that looked through the line of young
men, she said, "They object."

"To sleeping here? Because we're not married? I'm staying in another suite," he assured them. "My family owns the hotel. We have other rooms."

A snort from one of the men almost overrode what Jaya said, her voice quiet and uneven. "It's the marriage they don't support."

A quick blast of Punjabi came at her from her uncle.

She said something back, speaking firmly, but Theo could feel the tension in her was so acute she threatened to shatter.

"You're too rich, man," one of the young men blurted. "Look at my father. We can't pay a dowry that would keep you living like this." He waved at the opulence of the Makricosta Olympus suite. "Jaya should have known better than to agree. Are you that angry with our uncle you'd ruin him?" he demanded of her.

Jaya started to respond, but Theo gently squeezed her into silence, his fury nearly blinding him. It took everything he had to remain calm and civilized. He hated confrontation, but he'd been serious about fighting to the death for her.

"Dowries are illegal. I brought you here because Jaya wished to have her family at our wedding. If you leave, that will hurt her. I can't allow that." He held first her brother's gaze, then her uncle's.

Into the silence, her father said, "Jaya?" He patted Zephyr's leg and smiled.

Jaya drew a sharp breath and said, "Yes, he's mine." She drew Theo forward and crouched to the floor so it would be easier for her father to see her. She spoke slowly in Punjabi to him, something about their wedding and then she introduced Theo as her groom, straightening to stand beside him with pride.

Theo drew her close while the old man studied them. He felt on trial as he used the Punjabi he was still learning to ask her parents for their blessing.

She tilted her smile up to him, her pride in him almost too much to withstand.

When her father nodded, Jaya dissolved into happy tears, first kissing her father then wrapping her arms around Theo so tightly he could barely breathe.

He looked over her head at her brother, still twitching at all the animosity hovering in the room, but bearing it, for her. "I intend to take care of your parents. Leave if you wish, but if you'd like to hear the arrangements you should stay. Now, Jaya." He coaxed her to show her damp face. "Would you please introduce me to the rest of your family?"

As the days of celebration raged, Jaya agonized over whether it was too much for Theo. They hadn't gone with a full-out Indian wedding, but there was enough to be overwhelming.

That's why it surprised her he spent an hour with her male relatives without telling her. Then she was even more annoyed when her brother told her it had been about his arrangements for their parents.

"Every time Uncle raised an objection, Theo said, 'I thought of that, but...' Uncle underestimated him. We all underestimated you." He eyed her like he couldn't imagine how his disreputable sister had landed such a catch.

She quizzed Theo later on when he'd turned into a chauvinist and why he'd kept her from a meeting that impacted her.

"Two reasons," he said without apology. "First, I wanted your uncle to know that he can't manipulate you with guilt or fear any longer. You won't be padding his life with your earnings because I will provide your parents with their own home and income and a care aid for your father. If your uncle finds himself suffering financially, and needs to ask you for help, that will be at your discretion. You have the power now, not him."

"Oh." She was too overwhelmed by the sense of shackles falling off her body to know what else to say. "And the other reason?"

"I'm so angry with the way he treated you, I don't want you in the same room with him."

She didn't cross paths with her uncle much. All of them were so busy with the nearly two hundred guests that swelled the hotel to capacity. Cousins from both sides took over the two lower floors, work associates of the Makricostas' flew in from all four corners, and friends of Jaya's arrived wide-eyed with awe from Bali and Marseilles. Quentin and Bina were the last to arrive and Theo arranged for them to stay with his family, knowing there might be awkwardness with Jaya's.

It was a heart wrenching moment when Jaya's aunt, Saranya's mother, greeted Bina with open arms. Jaya grew tearful during the reception, recalling the way the little girl had broken down in her grandmother's arms, both of them united in grief. Bina had missed out on so much living in Saranya's exile, but her family connections were being restored now. Saranya would have been so happy.

"Jaya," she heard near her ear just before a broad hand settled on her waist and Theo's wide shoulders loomed to block out the Grand Ballroom. "Are you okay?"

She nodded and smiled through her tears. "Just wishing Saranya could be here to see how happy you've made me. You've given me back my family, Theo. They're healing rifts that have broken us apart for years. Thank you."

"I wanted that for you." His smile was so tender, she barely felt the knife of knowing he deliberately surrounded her with love from other sources so she wouldn't miss his.

"But you didn't expect all this, did you?" she said, sheepish at how she'd taken him at his word and put together a wedding that married their two cultures as well as themselves.

He glanced around the room draped in red silk curtains. Gold beads dangled in strings from the ceiling like sunlight caught in raindrops. Children were trying out the bride and groom's thronelike chairs under the floral covered *mandap.* Brilliant saris competed with designer gowns as people danced and stole exotic treats from the circulating waiters.

"This is definitely more socializing than I can typically swallow, but I'm not sorry. Everything is very beautiful." His gaze came back to her, his admiration evident in his slow, studied perusal. "Especially you. I don't know why I never pictured you like this, so exotic. You're breathtaking." His gaze paused on the pendant of her *maang tikka* dangling off the line of pearls in the part in her hair.

"You must feel like you've married a stranger." She lifted a hand to check her red-and-gold headscarf hadn't slipped. His gaze followed the sound of her abundant gold bangles clattering against the red and faux ivory ones anchored on her wrist. She felt like a pack mule, she wore so much heavy, ornate jewelry.

He looked striking himself, not wearing a turban or *pyjama,* but he was carrying a sword over his white morning coat.

"Thank you for including Adara and Rowan in the henna party. When they heard it was supposed to be only for the bride's family, they were devastated."

"They're my friends. Of course I would invite them." In truth, they were quickly becoming as close as sisters to her. "Did they tell you I could barely make it through having my feet painted?" All the women had bonded with laughter when it turned out Jaya's feet were so ticklish, she'd had to keep stopping the artist and making her work on others until she could withstand another few minutes of torture.

"They said my initials are hidden somewhere in the design. I can't wait to look for them." His smoky voice poured a wash of electric tingles over her.

She ducked her head, embarrassed by how badly she was anticipating being alone with him. Naked. It had been almost two years and so much had changed, her body, her feelings for him. They ran so deep now. If the henna artist was right about the color representing how intense her feelings for her husband were, her tattoos should last years.

He caressed the sensitive skin beneath her ear and along her nape, leaning in to ask, "When can we leave?"

A punch of unfettered desire clenched her middle. Her shoulder burned under the weight of his hand resting there. When he grazed his lips against her cheek her throat locked, she was so overcome by hunger.

"You're killing me," he said in a loaded voice. "Tell me. An hour? How much longer?"

She couldn't speak, could only lift her face so he could see how helpless she was to the feelings he incited in her. A muted ringing filled her ears and she realized it was her, trembling amid all this fine gold.

His tormented expression hardened into fierce excitement. *"Now."*

If he had swung her into his arms, she wouldn't have felt more swept away. He turned them toward the room and she wished they could disappear without speaking to anyone. This passion between them was nothing she felt shame over, but it was too personal and concentrated to endure a gauntlet of teasing over it.

Before they could move, Demitri lurched in front of them, unkempt, wearing a smear of lipstick on his cheek. "Hey, I'm ready to claim my dance with the bride."

"Too late," Theo said with only a hint of smugness. He waved away whatever Demitri tried to say. "Redeem yourself by making our excuses. We're leaving."

She thought Demitri might have tried to say something, but Theo stole her out a side exit. From there they broke into a run like schoolchildren and were both laughing and breathless when they tumbled into the elevator.

"We should at least say goodbye to Zephyr," she protested as Theo crowded her into a corner, his grin so boyish and lighthearted she grew dizzy.

"If there's any male getting more attention from women than my brother this week, it's our son. He won't miss us."

Curling his fists against the walls of the elevator, caging her in, he inhaled deeply without actually touching her, then growled in frustration when the elevator stopped, jarring them both into a small stagger.

"I know I'll appreciate the privacy once we get to Rosedale, but right now it's too damned far away." He pushed back and held the doors for her.

The wind had come up and whipped around them as they crossed to the helicopter. A uniformed pilot touched his cap as he helped Jaya up the stairs.

"You're not driving?" she asked Theo.

He gave her a look as he settled beside her in the passenger cabin. "We call it piloting," he drawled, accepting a glass of champagne from the flight attendant that he passed to Jaya, but declined for himself. He picked up her free hand and set a playful bite on the knuckle of her ring finger. "I knew I'd only be thinking of you at this point. Not the right headspace for getting us anywhere alive. This is Nic's crew. They make the trip all the time. Plus, all the pre-flights are done."

She saw the advantage to that as they lifted off the second her seat belt clicked into place. The attendant moved to the copilot's seat and lowered the lights. Minutes later they were high enough and far enough away that the city and sky blended into a blanket of pinprick lights. The moon sat fat and smiling a bluish glow.

Theo touched her chin, bringing her around from staring into the silver-laced waves and captured her mouth with the velvet heat of his. She opened to his pressure, tongue seeking the dampness of his, their union growing deep and wet between one startled breath and the next. Her hand sought the back of his head, urging him to kiss her harder as waves of delicious heat rolled down to the center of her, flooding sensations between her thighs, making her ache.

They were in another world, a bubble of white noise and shadow, straining against their belts as they twisted to be closer. She brushed at the lapel of his jacket, burrowing to his vest and seeking a way past it only to be thwarted by the silk of his shirt.

He groaned and skimmed his hand from her knee up her thigh, over her waist and cupped her breast, thumb circling over silk to tease her nipple. She wriggled in her seat, the erotic sensations building in her loins so intense she gasped and pulled away.

"Please stop."

"Damn, I'm sorry." He sat back, his face stark with self-recrimination as he closed his hands into fists on his armrests. "I misread you."

"No, you didn't." She threw her arm across him, face tilted against his shoulder so her whispered words could reach his ear over the din of the helicopter blades. "I'm afraid I'm going to…I can't. Not here, like this, with people right there who might know."

Theo's hands opened to clench into the ends of his armrests. She could feel the strain and flex in his biceps and across his chest as he nearly rent the crash-proof seats apart. His head tilted back and the sound he made was animalistic, somewhere between fury and helplessness.

When she started to pull back in alarm, he trapped her hand against his chest where his heart slammed. They sat like that until the bird landed on the lawn of a dark estate. An English mansion waited with stately patience, seeming out of place on this Greek island, but who cared? It was

Nic and Rowan's home, a gift of privacy for their wedding night, but Jaya barely saw any of it as Theo whisked her up the steps, past a housekeeper who said something about calling if they needed anything and practically booted her out the door.

"Are you cross? You seem angry," Jaya said, backing away from him in the dimly lit lounge.

"Because I almost lost it up there along with you? Hell, no, I'm going insane." He dragged at his clothes, shedding sword and bowtie and shoes as he stalked her. "Are you afraid of me right now?"

"What? No, not really, but—oh!" She came up against the bottom stair, surprised he'd steered her this way. "You seem really, um… What if the housekeeper comes back and finds your clothes all over the house like this?"

"She won't come back uninvited." His vest hit the floor. "Keep going." He jerked his chin at the upper floor, urging her to back up the stairs.

"You're kind of being, um…" She didn't know what the word was, but he was making her nervous. Not genuinely afraid, but she knew what a small animal felt like when stalked by a cat.

"Aggressive?" he prompted. "Impatient? I'm trusting you, my lovely bride. Keep going. One of these bedrooms is made up for us."

"Trusting me? To what?" She hurried down the hall ahead of him, sending anxious glances over her shoulder as he followed at an implacable pace. "What do you mean? Oh! It's so nice of them to do this…"

She entered an expansive bedroom where the scent of the sea wafted in through open balcony doors with the sensual push of each wave reaching for shore. Tea lights floated in glass globes of colored water, bringing a magical glow to the white sheets and sheer curtains around the canopied bed. An array of treats awaited on a side table beneath silver covers, but she didn't lift the lids, too aware of the half-naked man, his hands lowering his fly as he stepped through the door and left it half-open.

The low light burnished his muscled chest and flat stomach, accentuating his abs. She found herself shaking too much with excitement to be able to remove so much as her grandmother's heavy ring from her forefinger.

Theo moved toward her like he was a missile finding its target. His chest filled her vision and his aggressive masculine scent filled her nostrils, making her dizzy. Without thinking, she impulsively smoothed the narrow line of hair that arrowed down the center of his torso to his navel and lower to the exposed skin behind his loosened fly.

"I, um, don't know what you mean about trusting me," she said.

He sucked in a breath that pulled all his stomach muscles taut. He cupped the side of her face and made her look at him.

"I'm trusting you to tell me if I'm coming on too strong. Have you reached your limit? You're shaking."

"No! I want to touch you and be naked and feel you all over me but look at me! I can't get out of any of this on my own and—"

He kissed her, hard and fierce, the thrust of his tongue forceful, but so welcome, so good. She sucked on him, wanting to eat him alive. They'd been kissing and fondling and teasing for weeks. Her dreams had been full of how he felt thrusting inside her. She couldn't wait any longer. Modesty didn't enter into it. Instinct took over.

With a grunt of hunger he backed toward the bed and sat, pulling her to straddle his legs, gathering her sari and underskirt as he pulled her into his lap. She knelt with her knees parted to hug his hips. The position put her eye to eye with him, mouth to mouth. They never stopped kissing and she couldn't stop soaking in the feel of his skin with

her splayed hands. Tiny noises escaped her, like an abandoned kitten then more of a purr when his hot hands slid
up to cup the globes of her buttocks. She wriggled in his
hold, loving the intimacy of it, wanting him to know how
much pleasure his touch gave her.

Her whole body was filling with heat and excitement,
blossoming like a flower coated in dew and sunlight.

With a ragged moan, he snapped her underpants, surprising her into gasping and lifting in surprise. He tugged
them away and threw them to the floor then freed himself.
She reached for the thrusting flesh he revealed, circling
him with tentative fingers, reacquainting with the warm
satin over hot steel.

The world contracted to this small circle of light where
one man and one woman consummated their marriage,
harsh breaths mingling as she helped him roll on a condom.

Wordlessly he guided her to lift and be open for him. She
let her eyes drift closed as he guided his straining head to
rub and tease. Soft gasps of anticipation escaped her and
she dug her nails into his shoulders.

When she started to take him in, he gathered her swollen, aching breasts in two hard hands and bit through her
sari at her nipples, making her cry out and arch, desperate
for penetration. As she let her weight sink down, as her wet,
ready sheath swallowed him, he dropped his head back and
snarled at the ceiling.

Smiling, she scraped her nails across his chest and
worked herself to find the tightest fit against him, heart
expanding with joy at each pulse of his hard muscle inside
her. He dug his hands through silk to snug her tighter and
tighter still, causing delicate explosions as the right place
was touched again and again.

They kissed, deep, sumptuous kisses, rocking themselves into ownership of each other's body. Soon their
movements exaggerated, pulling away and coming to-

gether with more force. She had never ridden a horse, but she rode her husband, using her thigh muscles to rise and fall on exquisite impalement, feeling the strain in him as he balanced on the edge of the mattress, sweaty and strong beneath her, holding himself steady to let her set their pace. His breaths rang with strain and his chest and shoulder muscles bunched with tension. When her stamina began to fail, his hands grasped her hips and kept her rhythm steady so they approached the crisis together.

"Theo! I'm—" Her world was coming apart at the seams.

"Me, too. Now, Jaya. Let me feel you—ah, yes. Like that. Ah, yes, yes!"

She imploded then expanded like a supernova, his pulsing completion within her shooting her into a realm where they were one experience, one person. One.

Draped naked on her stomach across the bed, she lay acquiescent as her husband kissed and stroked his way around the henna on her feet and lower legs. Every few minutes he ran a playful fingertip down the sole of her foot or nuzzled too softly at her ankle—he almost got a reflexive kick in the eye for that one—but he was enjoying himself so she tried to withstand the tickling.

"Here," he finally said, kissing hotly inside her calf.

"Are you sure?" She sat up, scooping the edge of the sheet for a shred of modesty, then studied the scrolled *T.M.* "Should I have it tattooed there permanently?"

"Would you?" he asked. He was so sexy with his rakish stubble and relaxed grin, propped on an elbow and completely at ease in his nudity. He took her breath.

"If you'd like. Unless you have a different favorite spot?" The flirting came naturally after hours of physical contact that bordered on debauchery. They couldn't seem to get enough of each other, whether they were in the bed, against the shower wall, or on the sideboard. Morning was firmly coming alive outside. Birds sang and the air had gone from crisp to soft. The helicopter would be returning them to Athens by late afternoon, but they were very much still on their one-night honeymoon.

Lazy brown eyes perused her from hairline to toenails. "It's all my favorite."

"I never thought I'd be like this," she admitted. "Naked and comfortable with a man. I thought I'd have hang-ups forever. Thank you for making this so good for me." She tilted forward to touch her mouth to his.

"I'm not being too demanding? You would tell me if you're tender, wouldn't you? I look back on our night in Bali and it was incredible, but damn, I was stiff the next day. You should have told me to back off."

"Why didn't you put on the brakes?"

"Because I didn't want that night to end."

She smiled, feeling secretive and womanly and desired. "Neither did I."

"I've never had second chances before." He smoothed her hair behind her ear. The somber gratitude reflected in his eyes warmed her heart. "Don't let me screw this up. Tell me what I need to do to make this work, okay?"

Love me, she thought, feeling a pinch in her heart, but it wasn't something either of them could control. It would happen or not. Still, when he took his time caressing and kissing her, when their bodies writhed together in sensual perfection, she felt loved.

Seeking that, she eased onto her back, pulling him with her. "I'm the inexperienced one," she reminded. "You're supposed to be the one who knows how to make this work."

He flashed a grin, brief and endearingly playful. "If this is all I have to do, our marriage will be a cake walk."

CHAPTER THIRTEEN

FOR A MAN who had never wanted a wife and children, Theo was surprised how quickly he settled into marital bliss. Not that any of it was easy, but it wasn't hard in the way he knew life could be hard. It was little blips of leasing his New York apartment—it was too good an investment to sell outright—being away from Jaya and Zephyr because of a crisis in Sydney and managing child-care until the *au pair* arrived since Jaya was already getting her feet wet in her new job.

The flip side of these minor wrinkles was a smart, warm, stunning woman on his arm and in his life.

He wasn't a man who'd ever needed to bring the prettiest woman to the dance. Nevertheless, he'd had a roster of style conscious women who hadn't minded an evening out on short notice. He'd given them a shopping spree and they'd relieved him of the burden of conversation for a few hours.

Jaya elevated what he used to think of as endurance events to a new, very bearable level, bringing personality without getting too personal. Her people management skills made her the perfect hostess when they were forced to entertain. As a result, he found himself in the remarkable position of enjoying this evening's dinner.

Now that they were settled, she'd taken a job with the family business, choosing an upgrade project that would allow her to work closely with him. While some considered that a recipe for disaster, he had more faith. They tended to work like two halves of a whole and today had been no different, despite being a grueling one over all. However, they'd put their team in place and were kicking off the project with a dinner for spouses. It was also a soft opening for the revamped dining room in their centerpiece New York hotel.

"There will be times when we're asking your husband or wife to work late, so we wanted to let you know up front that we appreciate the sacrifice," Jaya was saying, her graceful fingers resting lightly on the edge of the white tablecloth. If she was nervous speaking to the long table of nearly thirty people, her boss included, she didn't betray it.

"We won't always be eating like this. I'm sure there will be sandwiches at midnight more often than not, but today was a very productive meeting and if we can keep up that momentum, we'll be enjoying another celebration like this at the end of a very successful project." With a teasing smile that impacted like a heart punch, she added to Theo, "Provided we're on budget, of course."

"You will be." Maybe he was biased, even a bit dazzled. He certainly wouldn't let her fail, but he had every confidence she'd pull this off beautifully.

"They're so in love," the wife of their IT specialist said, then pressed fingertips to her lips as everyone turned to look at her. "I'm sorry! I didn't mean to say that so loud."

She was mortified and everyone else seemed amused, but Theo felt as though he'd been stripped naked in front of all of them. Was that what this was? Love?

His sense of vulnerability, of having his deepest desire revealed, was so threatening he couldn't look at Jaya. It would only reinforce how much she meant to him, allowing others to wield his feelings for her as a weapon. He cut an instinctive glance to the place he'd always been able to count on for cover when he was at his least guarded.

Adara was already watching him and smoothly drew everyone's attention to her end of the table. "We're very excited about this pairing. Even if they weren't married, I would have wanted Jaya to head this project, but having them so closely connected should help you all get the answers you need so you can keep moving forward."

Gideon made some remark about the newlyweds curtailing their honeymooning to review software code, but Theo didn't absorb it. The luminescent curtain that surrounded them in this private dining area was supposed to give a waterfall effect, but he was drowning under the rapids at the moment. The pressure in his chest suffocated him while he tried to discern which way was up. Pressure in his ears made the room's music sound muted while the clink of crystal tableware was like shattering glass.

He was falling apart internally while he had to maintain an unaffected front, exactly as he always had.

Jaya was pretty sure she'd never be able to eat here again. She couldn't eat now, when an amuse-bouche arrived in the form of a tiny fried noodle nest with a grape tomato egg and a herb leaf feather floating in a spoonful of consume. She wanted to run away and hide from the terrible lie that she was allowing to prevail.

Her husband *didn't* love her. She wished he did. Every morning she woke next to him hoping today would be the day he'd find the words. In six weeks of marriage, no matter how happy they seemed on the surface, he had yet to speak of his feelings.

But she had to sit here and smile at a table of mostly strangers, reminding herself that her life was actually very fulfilling. Theo did care for her in his way. He had overturned his life for her and their child, provided for them in a way that was ridiculously extravagant and always made time for them.

Then there was the sex. As a couple, they might not be

given to public displays of affection, but behind closed doors they were the clichéd newlyweds who couldn't keep their hands off each other. They started most of their days locked in orgasm and fell asleep sweaty and tangled together.

So what did it matter if people assumed they were in love and it was only true on one side? She was still happy, wasn't she?

Don't be impatient, Jaya. Don't ruin it.

That was a bitter imperative to swallow when she'd spent the beginning of her life telling herself, *Go after what you want. Don't settle.*

The evening turned into the longest of her life and only became more intolerable when they said good-night to their guests at the coat room. Theo held her wool wrap and asked near her ear, "You okay?"

This from the man who had become Robot Theo for the last two hours, tense and barely able to string two civil words together, leaving all the talking to her. If she'd found the love remark disconcerting, he'd found it insufferable.

"I'm fine," she mumbled as she clutched the edges of the wrap across her aching breastbone.

Across the room, Gideon lifted Adara's hair out from beneath the collar of her jacket. His gaze on her was tender as he cupped her face to give her a light kiss. Her smile when he drew back was radiant.

Jaya wanted to cry. She'd settled and could never back out now, even if she hadn't loved her husband so much she thought she'd die of it.

"Don't lie to me, Jaya," he said beside her with quiet ferocity. "Even if you think it might be easier for both of us."

She met his gaze, but it was painful to hold. He'd see how much regret filled her. Funny how she'd thought the worst thing in the world had been being a financial burden on her uncle. No, it was far worse to be an emotional burden. She didn't want Theo to know she loved him when he couldn't love her back. It would be more weight on his conscience than he deserved to carry. It wasn't his fault he couldn't love.

"Adara," he called, startling Jaya with his sharp tone.

His sister turned back from exiting with her husband.

"Is something wrong?" she asked as she approached, looking between the two of them. The weird thing was, it was like she already knew. Jaya had a feeling Adara was as aware of how tonight's gaffe had affected Theo as Jaya was.

A gut-wrenching sense of rejection filled her as she saw Theo's not loving her blink larger than the sign in Times Square. Everyone knew.

"Will you swing by our place on your way home and take Zephyr overnight? The sitter can't stay," Theo said. "I'll text her to let her know."

"What? No!" Jaya protested in shock. "Why—?"

"Of course," Gideon cut in smoothly. "Our pleasure."

"But we're going straight home," Jaya insisted. "Aren't we?"

"We'll use the family suite here tonight."

"Theo—" Jaya began.

"Please let us do this." Adara set a light touch on her arm. "Theo never asks me for anything." Leaning in to buss Jaya's cheek with her own, she whispered, "Please don't give up on him." With a tight smile of concern, she and Gideon hurried away.

Speechless, Jaya watched them depart. "This is crazy. Why did you do that?"

"Crazy? We both know we need to talk."

She hugged herself into her wrap, cold despite their staying inside. As he nudged her toward the elevators, she stumbled.

"I don't want to talk," she mumbled. This was her problem, not theirs. She had known what she was marrying.

Maybe he would come to love her eventually, but not if she forced it.

"There's a switch." He eyed her as he brought out his card and got them into the private elevator.

"What is?"

"You being the one who doesn't want to talk. Especially after you taught me it's the only way to fix things. Why are you trying to take that away from me now?"

"I'm not," she protested as they entered the family suite. "I just don't see any use this time."

"Why not?"

"Because I don't want to hear *again* that you don't love me and never will!" The outburst surprised even her. She pulled her wrap tighter around her throat, turning away to hide her hurt.

He drew a long, harsh breath then heavy silence descended.

She waited.

Nothing.

A choking little cry of protest escaped her. "And there you go again, withdrawing—"

"It's not easy for me, Jaya! I don't even know how to love, not properly. I still feel awkward kissing my son, like the more I want and need him in my life, the more likely he'll be snatched away."

"Not by me! I'm not trying to take away your heart either. Love isn't something to *dread.*"

"I know that," he cut in. "But people knowing how I feel... When that woman said we were in love tonight, I lost a bit of sanity. I couldn't bear for them to know how much you mean to me. It makes me too vulnerable."

It wasn't the statement she was looking for, but it was close enough to make her turn and look at him. "Do you mean that?"

"The last thing I feel toward you is dread, Jaya. When I

walk through the door, I'm relieved, like some kind of un-
identified pain has stopped. I'm so damned happy to see
you, it's embarrassing. Is that love? You tell me. I've never
felt like this toward anyone. It sure as hell isn't anything
like what I feel toward my sister," he growled.

She pressed a hand to her diaphragm, reminding herself
to keep breathing because she felt as though the wind had
been knocked out of her. Somehow she found her voice.
"Each time I see you, I'm filled with intense *joy*, like I'm
finally home and safe again, no matter where we are."

Reaction seemed to spasm across his features. "When
you say things like that, I almost don't want to believe it.
It means too much and I trained myself not to care, not to
want, but I crave those things you say, Jaya. They make
me start to hope."

"For what?" A fragile bubble of optimism was building
in her, but she was afraid to grasp it in case it burst.

He visibly struggled, feet shifting, glance cutting to the
door before he hardened his stance and lifted his chin,
no defenses anywhere on him as he revealed both somber
vulnerability and an achingly tender warmth toward her.

"That you might come to love me one day."

Her own controls fell away, leaving her floating in a
void, jaw slack, mind wiped clean by shock. A hot pressure flared in the back of her throat, urging her to speak,
but all she could say was, "I'm such an idiot."

Before she could cover her face and absorb how appall-
ingly stupid she'd been, she glimpsed how her words affected him. The tightening and closing, the dimming of
his eyes.

"I thought if I told you how much I love you, it would
scare you," she blurted, lurching forward a step. "I'd make
you feel too much pressure. Like you were failing me because we're not equal, but I shouldn't have held back. I
should have told you."

"That you love me," he clarified in a voice that rocked between disbelief and shaken anticipation. He came forward to grasp her arms. "That's what this is? This feeling like if we have a disagreement, I'll die of loneliness? That if I'm hurting I don't want anyone around except you, and if you're there I can bear anything, that's it? That's love?"

She nodded, blinking matted lashes. A tickle of wetness ran onto her cheek. "That's how it is for me. I want to tell you things I'd never admit to another soul."

He cupped her face in gentle fingers, his eyes blazing with heat and admiration and adoration. "Then Jaya, I have loved you for a very long time."

She couldn't breathe. Her heart had grown too big for her chest. Her mouth wouldn't form words because her lips were quivering.

He soothed them with the pressure of his own. The tender kiss deepened by degrees past sweet wonder into heat and passion and a deep need to express their love completely. They knew each other's signals and they were even more evocative now. He cupped her breast and held her heart. She pressed her lips to the pulse in his throat and only a very fine, translucent wall separated her from his lifeblood.

"Oh, Theo, I'm sorry—"

"Shh, I shouldn't have made you wait, either. I just didn't know…"

"I know. I love you." She kissed him again, unable to control the outpouring of emotion, passion, her need to connect.

He slowly drew back, but only to offer a smug smile. "I scored us a free night of babysitting."

"How could I not love you for that?" She was bursting with joy at how carefree he looked. Like he'd fully broken free of his shell and all of him was available to her.

He swooped to whisk her off her feet and into the cradle of his arms, making her gasp in surprise. As he started for the bedroom, she toed off her shoes so they clunked to the floor.

"Are we going to sleep at all tonight?" she teased.

"You say when, you know that." He set her onto the bed and followed her in one motion, his strength and power entwining with hers in the familiar way she'd come to love. "But I'll make it worth staying up if you do," he cajoled.

He did, fulfilling her completely when, hours later, they were trembling with sexual exhaustion. Still panting, damp skin adhered and bodies locked in ecstasy, he smoothed her hair from her cheek with a shaking hand and looked into her eyes. "I love you. I will love you forever. Thank you for being my wife."

* * * * *

Mills & Boon® Hardback
June 2014

ROMANCE

Ravelli's Defiant Bride	Lynne Graham
When Da Silva Breaks the Rules	Abby Green
The Heartbreaker Prince	Kim Lawrence
The Man She Can't Forget	Maggie Cox
A Question of Honour	Kate Walker
What the Greek Can't Resist	Maya Blake
An Heir to Bind Them	Dani Collins
Playboy's Lesson	Melanie Milburne
Don't Tell the Wedding Planner	Aimee Carson
The Best Man for the Job	Lucy King
Falling for Her Rival	Jackie Braun
More than a Fling?	Joss Wood
Becoming the Prince's Wife	Rebecca Winters
Nine Months to Change His Life	Marion Lennox
Taming Her Italian Boss	Fiona Harper
Summer with the Millionaire	Jessica Gilmore
Back in Her Husband's Arms	Susanne Hampton
Wedding at Sunday Creek	Leah Martyn

MEDICAL

200 Harley Street: The Soldier Prince	Kate Hardy
200 Harley Street: The Enigmatic Surgeon	Annie Claydon
A Father for Her Baby	Sue MacKay
The Midwife's Son	Sue MacKay

0514GEN STD HB

Mills & Boon® Large Print
June 2014

ROMANCE

A Bargain with the Enemy	Carole Mortimer
A Secret Until Now	Kim Lawrence
Shamed in the Sands	Sharon Kendrick
Seduction Never Lies	Sara Craven
When Falcone's World Stops Turning	Abby Green
Securing the Greek's Legacy	Julia James
An Exquisite Challenge	Jennifer Hayward
Trouble on Her Doorstep	Nina Harrington
Heiress on the Run	Sophie Pembroke
The Summer They Never Forgot	Kandy Shepherd
Daring to Trust the Boss	Susan Meier

HISTORICAL

Portrait of a Scandal	Annie Burrows
Drawn to Lord Ravenscar	Anne Herries
Lady Beneath the Veil	Sarah Mallory
To Tempt a Viking	Michelle Willingham
Mistress Masquerade	Juliet Landon

MEDICAL

From Venice with Love	Alison Roberts
Christmas with Her Ex	Fiona McArthur
After the Christmas Party...	Janice Lynn
Her Mistletoe Wish	Lucy Clark
Date with a Surgeon Prince	Meredith Webber
Once Upon a Christmas Night...	Annie Claydon

0514 GEN STD LP

Mills & Boon® Hardback

July 2014

ROMANCE

MEDICAL